Artemis

Karina Miller

Contents

Chapter One

"EMMETT—EMMETT, WAIT!"

The black-haired earl stopped mid-stride to turn to face his twin, his lips turning upwards into a gentle curve of a smile. The corners of his eyes crinkled lovingly as he regarded his sister.

"What is it, Linnie?"

Emmett Lockhart was, doubtlessly, a handsome man. His neatly-cropped hair was jet-black, a trait he had received from his late mother. His eyes were an emerald green inherited from his father. He was tall and well-built, and his long legs and strong arms rendered him excellent at dancing. At twenty and three he was earl to a large estate, and his riches combined with his appearance meant that he never had to worry over a lack of female attention.

"Before you go," Emmeline Lockhart panted, exhausted by the exertion of picking up her skirts and running across the courtyard to chase after her brother, all the while clutching onto the parcel she just had to deliver, "take this." She stuffed the square box (with a length half the length of a horse's head) wrapped in brown paper into Emmett's hand. Normally she would never have run the way she had, but judging from the wide distance between her and her twin coupled with the waiting carriage, she had no choice if she wanted to reach him in time.

Her brother accepted the box with a wry smile, but regarded it with a curious lift of his brow. "What is this, dear sister?"

"Just something for the road – something to eat in case you get hungry," she said, still breathless. "It... I made it myself."

"I appreciate the sentiment. I'm certain I will enjoy it." Emmett's smile stretched into a grin. "I will add, however, that I shall feel thoroughly let down if it isn't a slice of your wonderful blueberry pie."

Emmeline smiled shyly. "I suppose you shall just have to see it for yourself."

"Take care, Linnie," he said, his gaze soft upon his dearest relative in the world. "I know I will miss you most terribly, but know that I shan't be gone long – I promise I will be back not more than a fortnight from now."

"You have nothing to worry about," she assured him as she dropped into a deep curtsey. Although she was close with Emmett, she was taught in her most formative years by her strict governess to have a strong sense of propriety. She was not a lady by nature, one could say, but she would often hear Miss Paltrow's shrill voice by her ear reminding her sharply that she was a young lady, daughter of a duke, and should behave as such. "Stay safe, Emmett."

"Oh, let's not have any of this nonsense today. I imagine I will be sick with all this decorum when I am with Father in London for two weeks," he said with a light laugh. "Come here, dearest, and hug me goodbye."

When the siblings were alone with each other the titles of Lady and Earl often fell away together with the rest of the frivolities of high society, and Emmeline was more than glad to comply. The siblings briefly exchanged a tight embrace before Emmett dropped a kiss on her forehead and sighed regretfully. "I really must be on my way now. Ridiculous as it is at such short notice, Father expects me in London by luncheon tomorrow."

The girl's emerald eyes sparkled as she smiled somewhat teasingly at her brother. "Well then, Godspeed, and send Father all my love."

"I shall," he promised, reaching out to grasp her hand and squeezing it once. "Please make sure the dogs do not starve in my absence. I have instructed John to feed them every day, but I would be greatly reassured if my dearest sister herself could make sure John has fed them by supper."

She smiled, a trace of wickedness flashing past her eyes. "Of course."

"Don't you dare spoil them whilst I am away," he said. Although he meant to be stern with his sister, who liked to feed the sled dogs more than they should have to eat and make them too fat to be sled dogs just because food made them "so happy", he couldn't keep the grin from breaking out across his face.

Emmeline sighed melodramatically. "Very well, brother, if you must ruin my happiness, I suppose you may have my word." She paused as another idea appeared in her mind. "May I take the dogs out walking?"

"You're such trouble, Emmeline – will you ever grow up?" Emmett scolded, but his words were gentle. "I suppose you may, but only if you are escorted by John and your maid in waiting."

She rolled her eyes, something she would only ever do in front of her brother. "You know that that would be unnecessary, brother. I promise to stay within your property at all times."

He shook his head resignedly. "I know, but a proper young lady like you of all people should understand the importance of propriety."

She pouted, but nodded. Propriety. Of course. "I do understand." Then she offered him a warm smile. "I shan't delay you any more than I have, Emmy. Do be on your way to meet with Father, and if you're late, I would be more than happy to testify that it was all my doing."

"I would not let you take the fault for my choice to stay and talk."

"You couldn't possibly have left your sister dearest all alone without the goodbye she deserves," Emmeline disagreed with a playful grin. "Besides, Father would never fault me for anything. I'm a woman – according to him, anyway, I know no better and Father is such a just man that he'd never blame me for anything."

"Father can be a bigot," Emmett announced, "but I suppose we may use that to our advantage. You have all my love, Linnie." He lifted his sister's hand to his lips and pressed a loving kiss to it.

"As you have mine," she responded with a smile, squeezing her brother's hand affectionately, "but let me hold you back no longer. You must go this instant or Father shall have your head."

And so he turned, freshly-baked blueberry pie in hand, and jogged to the waiting carriage.

Despite the smiles they both sported, both Lockhart twins knew that it would be a long two weeks.

***

EMMELINE WAS NEVER BEAUTIFUL.

Everyone assumed that the dashing Earl of Portsmouth's fraternal twin must have been some kind of ravishing beauty. Upon first mention of Emmett Lockhart's unmarried sister, a person unacquainted with Emmeline's situation was quick to infer that the daughter of the Duke of Mayfair was simply so beautiful that she had the capacity to be choosy and hesitant with her suitors. They were always taken aback when they met her, because she...was not.

Emmeline was plain. She was not ugly, which she was grateful for, but she occasionally wished she was as beautiful as her mother had been, or as good-looking as her father and brother were. It made no sense to her – everyone in her bloodline had some kind of uncommon beauty about them, but by some trick of nature she looked no different from the lowest peasant. She had nothing against the common folk – she was well-acquainted with some – but some days she hated how she resembled not just a commoner but a beggar on the street. She hated how not a single man had ever cast her a second glance, how she was still unmarried at such a ripe age. Although her green eyes were the colour of gemstones and shone when she felt happy, she lacked the large round eyes most of her peers had. Her nose was not tall and aristocratic but a short snub, and her mouth was small and her lips thin. Her raven-black hair fell at her waist, but the strain of supporting such length had made it grow thin and frizzy. Skinny from birth, she lacked the curves needed to draw a man's gaze, and her bosom though tolerably rounded was far from full.

"My lady?" the lady's maid, who was trying to run a brush through her tangled locks, murmured softly from behind her as she sat at her vanity.

"Yes?"

"I know—I know it is not my place to ask, but I was just, I was just wondering...if you'd like to share the thing—share whatever's on your mind." The girl mustn't have been over ten and five. Her voice shook as if anticipating some fierce rebuke, and Emmeline could not help but smile slightly at her considerateness.

"You are very kind to ask, Penny, pray do not fear me so," Emmeline said in a kind, elder-sisterly tone she did not use often as youngest in the family. "I was fretting over the tangles in my hair. It's always such a struggle to brush through in the mornings."

"If you do not mind it, my lady, I might have a solution," Penny offered. "You see, my mother is a hairdresser, and she once saw a customer who had hair like yours – thick by nature but damaged by strain. She has a kind of oil that you can rub over your hair that might help. It worked wonders for that customer of hers, and from what I can tell of your hair, it might work for you, too."

"Oh! I should be most pleased if you could procure me a portion," Emmeline replied, smiling to herself at the thought of a remedy for her insufferable hair. "I shall hand you the money for it – just let me know how much I owe her."

"I certainly will be most glad to obtain you a bottle, my lady. But my mother thinks the world of you, you know, and I imagine she would be beyond delighted to supply you with some free of charge."

"You say your mother thinks the world of me, Penny?" Emmeline asked, her eyebrows lifting in flattery and astonishment. "She hasn't even met me. Whatever have I done to deserve her high esteem?"

Penny laughed, and Emmeline noticed how the young lady's maid's nervousness melted away at the mention of her mother. "Oh, she asks me about my work every time I go home for the holidays. I don't credit you any less than you deserve, and she believes as ardently as I do that you, my lady, are one of a kind for noble blood."

Emmeline smiled. "I, one of a kind? For noble blood? Truly, you and your mother are terribly sweet women, Penny, but I cannot concur with that."

"Oh, my lady, you credit yourself far too little." Penny started pulling her hair into a tight braid. "You are intelligent and kind and unbelievably thoughtful. You are the best sister I have ever seen, and, as far as I know, the least condescending lady there has ever been."

Emmeline murmured some polite answer that denied any positive trait about herself, in the way that the twisting feeling in her stomach always told her to do although her governess had always encouraged her to be vocal about her strengths. All Penny could do was laugh in a light fashion and hum, resignedly, "oh, my lady" because there was nothing else to be said that could possibly persuade the young woman that she was worth much more than she believed.

***

EMMELINE SAT BY THE WINDOW IN HER BEDROOM, WISH-ING THAT THE fourteen days till her brother's return would go by quicker than the one morning she had just endured had. Without his familiar presence and enjoyable company seconds seemed to stretch out into minutes, minutes into hours, and hours into entire eternities. Within the self-multiplying time that had gone by since Emmett's departure, she had already spent two hours sewing, three reading, and one on luncheon. She had been staring out the window and looking upon the courtyard for a while now (she lost track ten minutes in), boredom setting in like a latent illness that would eat at her bones, slowly corroding her mind, until she lost herself altogether in a dreamlike state similar to the inebriation she sometimes found Emmett in after dinner parties where a tad too much liquor had been served.

Sighing, she slid off the plush chair she had been perched on and milled about her room. There had to be something she could do, she thought as she paced restlessly. Perhaps she could go riding? No, that was an activity she saved for enjoying with Emmett, as the siblings' shared love of horses and speed meant that they saddled their stallions up and raced into the small wood near Emmett's property every Friday morning. Emmett would no doubt be disappointed to find out that she had gone without him in his absence.

Emmeline eventually decided to proceed to the music room and practise playing the violoncello. Although not many young ladies played the large bass violin like she did (if any at all, for she knew none who played), and despite the fact that she was not exceedingly skilled at the instrument, she enjoyed resting her hands against the large fingerboard and pulling the bow to produce the most beautiful sounds fraught with the deepest emotion. Hardly anyone knew that she was able to play it, with the exception of her brother and the household staff, and – despite her high opinion of propriety – she thrived off the ability to do something for herself, for her own happiness and not for the sake of prim and proper prettiness.

She played for hours, sending the deep and almost mournful melodies echoing across the house. The servants downstairs heard her and ex-changed knowing smiles. She would be late for tea, or perhaps even the evening meal – the young Lady Emmeline became late for many things once she became caught up in playing her violoncello. While Emmeline's governess had, many times in her childhood, insisted that the girl would like all music and would be far more well-versed in the pianoforte than in "that large, cumbersome instrument highly unfit for any proper lady, Emmeline I forbid you to play it", she could not help but find herself particularly favouring the gigantic stringed instrument and would only forget herself playing it. In front of the pianoforte she was acutely aware of the time, and although she had sufficiently persuaded herself that she enjoyed playing the instrument, she found herself waiting for her first opportunity to jump away from it.

Emmeline's lady's maid, Penny, who had been in the midst of running a bath for her lady, promptly stopped her work when she heard the music. Any hot water she managed to get into the bath would be ice cold by the time Emmeline was done, especially at this time of the year when the leaves were beginning to fade and fall. They were turning from the lush green the the earl thought likeable to the hues of red and orange and yellow and brown the lady adored, and soon temperatures would drop much more than they already had. Penny left Emmeline's bathroom to, instead, pick out another dress for the lady to wear for the rest of the day. She had just laid a blue dress on the young lady's bed, thicker than Emmeline's summer dresses to accommodate the cold weather, when one of the new butlers, clearly still young and inexperienced, hurried – nearly tumbled, in his mad rush – through the service door of Emmeline's room, a heap of formal wear and panicked expressions.

"Miss Penny," he breathed. "Thank goodness. Would you—Where is Lady Emmeline?"

Penny smiled, not hiding her amusement at the young man's flustered state. "Well, I would think the sound of the violoncello is a decent indication."

"There's a visitor, for Lord Portsmouth," the butler blurted out, clearly paying no attention to Penny's sarcastic remark. "His Lordship wasn't expecting him, and judging from the way she seems entirely absorbed in her playing, neither was the lady. He's asking a great deal of questions, and nobody quite knows what to tell him – we couldn't very well just tell him she's playing a violoncello, you know how you have to sit when you—"

"I understand, it hardly seems proper for a young lady," Penny cut in hurriedly. "Is he in the drawing room?"

"Currently, yes."

"Very well. Run and fetch him a pot of tea, and I will meet with you there."

***

Chapter Two

CAPTAIN PETER JAMISON WAS THOROUGHLY CONFUSED.

Upon arriving at his best friend's home he had learned that the Earl was away. When he asked nobody in particular where that lovely music was coming from, all the servants attending to him had grown flustered, hemming and hawing but not really saying anything. A long series of covert whispers had been exchanged right in front his eyes, as if he was not just standing there, before a young butler was shoved out a service door in a flurry. The music stopped shortly after, and the same butler who had been shooed out of the room rushed back in with a full pot of tea, which he nearly dropped before he set it down. He poured a cup and handed it to the captain, who, despite his bewilderment at how peculiar it was that all the servants seemed to anxious about something everyone but him knew, accepted the drink with a gracious word of thanks.

Sipping on the cup of Earl Grey, he was just beginning to wonder if he should just leave and call again another day when he saw Emmeline Lockhart walk through the door, presumably to meet her guest on behalf of her brother. She was tall and slim, an air of elegance about her as she floated into the room in a beautiful green dress. Although there was nothing remarkable about her features, Captain Jamison noted, she had some intangible beauty – something he occasionally noticed when she curtsied to him in the hallways of the Lockhart house and he bowed back, but stood out to him more now than ever because for the first time she would be having a proper conversation with him instead of remaining a woman he passed by in the hallway.

She nodded assuringly at the head butler, whose terse shoulders finally relaxed. He was not familiar with her and had never actually held a proper conversation with her although they had exchanged polite bows and curt-sies whenever they ran into each other when the captain called on the earl for a hunt or a game of cards. Captain Jamison tried to keep the bemused smile off his face as he stood to greet the Earl's sister, who had swept into one of the lowest curtsies he had ever seen.

"Good afternoon, Captain Jamison," she said with a welcoming smile once she had risen, "you are well? I believe the last time I had the pleasure of seeing you was...a month ago?"

"Yes, my lady, you have an excellent memory – I was here to join Emmett on a hunt. I have fared excellently since then, thank you," the Captain answered, nodding politely as he lifted Emmeline's hand to kiss it in the customary greeting. "Oh, yes. I was hoping to enquire after that beautiful music I heard a while ago. The servants did not seem able to produce an answer."

She didn't bat an eyelash. "Of course, Captain. I hired a violoncello player for a brief session – I do love music, you know, all kinds. I really would invite you and sit and listen with me, but unfortunately he was scheduled to leave shortly after you arrived and I have sent him off a tad early."

"I see. Fret not, my lady, I play the violoncello myself and I may listen to it whenever I please." Captain Jamison smiled courteously. "Have you had your tea, my lady?"

Emmeline smiled back, her eyebrows lifting in pleasant surprise. Yet she did not comment on his ability to play the violoncello, which in truth was the only thing he'd said that she took interest in. "I'm afraid not; I was thoroughly enthralled by the music, I love it so. Would you care to stay for some? We have some excellent tea leaves Emmett bought during his last escapade – he says they were grown in the mountains, you know, and I hear the chef will be preparing some excellent French macarons today. It would be a dreadful shame not to share such a delightful meal."

Captain Jamison smiled at her. "Why, macarons are my favourite, Lady Emmeline, and I hope you do not regret telling me about them because now you shall not be able to be rid of me till tea is over."

"Truly, Captain?" Emmeline said melodramatically with an exaggerated clasp of her hands as she sensed his joking tone. "Oh, whatever have I done!"

He laughed, a deep and rumbling in his chest. She beamed at him, and no more words needed to be exchanged between the two as they found new friends in one another. Neither had expected to get along so well with the other, since the only thing they had in common was Emmett Lockhart.

"Shall we have tea in the parlour, Captain?" Emmeline offered eventually. "I believe the chef should have everything set up."

Captain Jamison nodded and rose with her. Her lady's maid and the head butler John trailing behind her, she led him through the halls, and he noticed how light her steps were in contrast with the heavy clunk of men's boots on wooden floorboards he was so used to. He was almost tempted to ask if she had any feet at all, or if she simply floated, but he knew it was a stupid question and wisely decided to avoid making himself look like a grand oaf.

Instead, he inquired after her brother. "You are excellent company, my lady, but I've been meaning to ask – wherever has Emmett gone?"

Emmeline laughed at his caution. She was not some fragile porcelain doll that would shatter upon the lightest touch, and she certainly did not expect to be treated as such. "Oh, Captain, I assure you I do not take offence thus easily. My brother is on his way to London to meet with my father."

"London!" he exclaimed, slapping a hand to his forehead. "Why, I just missed him then, I was there just two days ago!"

"Emmett will, however, return within the fortnight," she said with an apologetic smile, as if she had to be sorry for the unhappy coincidence. "Perhaps you may call again then."

"Perhaps I may call again before then," Captain Jamison said, quite nearly blurting it out, the words slipping out of his mouth before he even realised what he was saying. Both parties turned bright red immediately. Having spent much time on his ship and not having much contact with females at all, he had not yet gotten used to flirting with women and was shy and awkward when he did so although he was already of age twenty and four; and Emmeline, despite having excellent dowry, had features that were merely tolerable and was beyond unaccustomed to male attention of a remotely romantic or flirtatious nature.

"Perhaps," Emmeline managed to finally say, "you could come with me when I walk Emmett's sled dogs tomorrow." She paused before hurriedly adding, "The butler and my maid in waiting will be with us, of course, and we will stay within the property. We wouldn't want to encourage any tongues to wag."

"That sounds...enjoyable," Captain Jamison replied, sounding quite like the awkward adolescent boy he once was. Perhaps part of that fumbling young man still remained in him, despite the new air of confidence and strong leadership he had found at the helm of his ship.

"Surely it will be now that I shall be accompanied by a friend," the girl beside him offered with a hopeful smile. She could not be romantically involved with this man. Emmett himself had warned her of her fate if she married him. He was a sailor, an ambitious navy-man, already a captain at only twenty and four. He was often away on various expeditions that his career mandated he embark on for weeks at a time. Emmeline was aware that, for the past month, he had vanished away to the colony half a world away in the East Indies as part of a fleet securing the local waters. These trips happened frequently, Emmett had told her, and if she married him, she would find herself frequently without a husband again. He would someday climb the ranks, and these disappearances were only likely to become more commonplace. She would take her brother's advice – she always did; but though Captain Peter Jamison was not suitable to be a suitor to her, they did get along beautifully, and could become a treasured friend.

Captain Jamison returned her smile, a hint of apology in his eyes. He regretted his words as much as she did. He too thought that they were probably better suited as platonic friends, at least for the moment being. "Well, my lady, I think you're absolutely right."

"Splendid," Emmeline cheered, glad and relieved that they had finally gotten past that awkward moment and reached an understanding about how their relationship would play out. "Now, Captain, I may not be able to speak on your behalf, but I am ravenous and the macarons are straight ahead."

***

"THANK YOU SO MUCH FOR TEA, MY LADY."

"No thanks are needed, Captain Jamison," Emmeline assured him, the way that eyes shone telling him that her words were no mere courtesy. "The pleasure was all mine, and besides, you know my brother would all but have my head if I did any less than invite you to stay for a bite." She paused, pursing her lips in thought. The corners of her mouth stretched upwards into a broad grin, the kind Emmeline's governess proclaimed "no true lady ever shows, Emmeline – Lady Emmeline, you must cease doing that right this instant", as she spoke again. The mention of her brother often made her grin so, Captain Jamison had noticed. They must have been every bit and more as close as they appeared to the public eye.

"Actually, I think he'd still be utterly disappointed with me because I haven't made you sit down with me for a game of cards."

Captain Jamison laughed. It was true. Emmett Lockhart was well-known across the kingdom for his excessive hospitality, and many of the other nobles thought him a close friend because of it. While his father William Lockhart thought it foolish to be as generous as he was, the young earl's kindness had blessed him with an edge above many due to the connections he established.

"No, no, I'm not quite one for cards. Tea itself was fantastic, and you are a lovely person to dine with," he assured her. Like her brother, she had been an excellent host, though perhaps slightly shier and less expressive of her overflowing love and generosity. Emmett, however, was an extreme in this respect, and to the captain, Emmeline seemed just right.

"As are you. I had a wonderful time," Emmeline replied, a gentle smile continuing to grace her lips. It was, to the Captain, as if she was always happy – her eyes sparkled when she listened and when she spoke, her lips always sported a grin or a smile or a trace of a convex curve. He noticed that eyes turned a shade brighter still as she remembered something else. "Oh, yes, Captain, pray do not forget our appointment tomorrow. I find that I quite look forward to it."

"I promise I shall be here promptly at three, my lady."

"I will hold you to your word," she said almost like a warning, but the laughter in her eyes kept the mood light. He chuckled once more and nodded.

She curtsied and he bowed, laying a gentle kiss on her knuckles. Final niceties exchanged, they said one more goodbye for good measure and the captain turned and walked, in long strides, to his carriage, where a footman opened the door for him. Emmeline watched as he nodded in curt thanks and stepped onto the carriage, the muscle of his powerful shoulders visible through his jacket as he hoisted himself into the small box. Her eyes followed the carriage until it disappeared over the rolling hill, and when she could see him no longer her brow furrowed slightly as she wondered what on earth this high-ranking navy official might possibly see in a girl like her.

"Would you like your coat, my lady?"

Penny's soft voice cut through her reverie, and she turned to the maid in waiting and shook her head with a smile. "No, thank you, Penelope. I will be indoors in a minute. Run a bath for me, will you, and seek me in the music room when you're done."

The young girl bobbed a curtsy and was off. Emmeline let her eyes run over the beautiful view right outside her brother's main gate one last time before turning back into the house herself, letting the door click quietly shut behind her as she picked up her skirts and hurried back to the music room, where her violoncello had been waiting for too long.

***

"HERE YOU ARE, SIGNORINA, YOUR FAVOURITE," THE CHEF ANNOUNCED, sliding full plate in front of Emmeline. "Pasta, al dente, with chicken and funghi."

"Thank you very much, Adalberto." She beamed down at her food, eager to tuck in.

He stood back. "Is there anything else you require this evening, Signorina?"

"No, thank you." Emmeline looked up at him, still smiling. "But tell me, what did you think of the gentleman who came in at tea?"

"Oh, Capitano Jamison?" he clarified, his features brightening slightly. When she nodded, he grinned at her. "Sì, I have seen him with Lord Lockhart many a time – in fact, I served him lunch during his last visit. In my humble opinion at least, he is an excellent man, gracious and kindly, Signorina." He paused, a wry smile coming upon his face. "Why do you ask, do you take interest?"

Emmeline laughed. "I'm not sure, Adalberto. He and Emmett are close, you know, like brothers. Fratelli. It might be strange if I were involved with him in...in that fashion. It's difficult for me to envision us as any more than friends – you understand what I mean. Besides, my brother has spoken to me about this before... He thinks Captain Jamison cannot make me happy, because of his work. I think he is a wonderful man, but Emmett might not be happy if we courted, or..." A scarlet blush rose quickly to stain her cheeks, and Adalberto laughed.

"What, Signore Emmett instructed you not to grow fond of the Capitano?"

"Yes," she answered with a sigh. "He said that Captain Jamison is unable to bring me happiness... He claims that I will be one of the women who is always waiting for her husband to come home should I marry him. But Emmett is only ever concerned for me and my best interests, Adalberto;

will he not be upset if he knows that I have so directly disobeyed him, despite the fact that he was only trying to ensure my blissful future? Besides... What if he is right?"

"The Signore makes a valid point, but always remember – l'amore vince sempre," Adalberto said, his warm honey-golden eyes eyes twinkling kindly. Love conquers all. His eyes held all the warmth and wisdom of a father Emmeline never had. "I'm sure His Lordship will not be a problem. You know how much he loves you, Signorina. I doubt that he would stand in the way of love, if you really think you might love the Capitano."

"Truly, you think so?"

"I do," he assured her.

Before he left, he graced her with the same parting words that had formed one of the guiding principles of Emmeline's life – the same words he had said to her since she was a little girl, when there was still a Signora in the house. Now the Signora was gone, taken by illness far too early for her daughter to even remember her leaving, and a new one had come of age, but Emmeline would never quite be a grown woman in Adalberto's eyes. She would always be the piccola signorina to him. And so every day he would continue to remind her to eat well, laugh often, and love much, as her mother had taught him to do a long time ago when she had persuaded her father to employ a young Italian boy who had sincerely believed he would not have a second chance. It was with a fond smile on his lips that he once again reminded her of the mantra he lived by, the mantra Emmeline herself had grown to believe in.

"Mangia bene, ridi spesso, ama molto, Signorina."

"Sempre, Adalberto; sempre."

***

Chapter Three

E MMELINE PRACTICALLY FLEW DOWN THE STAIRS WHEN SHE HEARD THE carriage roll into the estate, rattling slightly along the cobblestone driveway. Once she had broken her fast that morning, she had bathed and washed her hair. Then she had instructed Penny to put her hair up in a neat bun and dress her in her favourite chartreuse dress specially designed for the autumn outdoors and her best walking boots. She wore a sparkling diamond necklace that had originally been her mother's, with a matching gold ring also inherited from the same late Lady Anne Lockhart. Emmeline was, without a doubt, looking her very finest. She was fully aware of the fact that she wanted to impress Captain Jamison. She avoided thinking of the motives behind this desire.

She was standing ready by the door, gloved hand tucked in gloved hand and a brilliant smile on her face, when Peter Jamison climbed off the carriage. He was dressed in a most handsome black suit with a cravat across his neck, something Emmeline noticed he did not normally sport. She smiled to herself, a crimson blush spreading down her cheeks to her neck, as she thought of the young officer trying to impress her as she was trying to do to him. She suppressed the burning sensation on her cheeks as he ascended the steps, one foot landing lightly in front of the other and hardly touching the granite such that he was nearly running to greet her.

"Good afternoon, my lady." Captain Jamison laid a kiss on her hand, and it pleased her more than a bouquet of fresh roses could have. "You are well?"

"I am very well, Captain," she responded, dropping into the lowest curtsy she could manage. "Better now that you have arrived."

The captain allowed himself a loud laugh, bowing to her in return. "As am I."

She offered him a slightly shy smile as she paused briefly before informing him that the stable boy would be along with the dogs soon. "I love the dogs," she told him. "They're absolute darlings."

"Indeed, it is hard not to build connections with them," he agreed. "I find myself quite fond of Jackie. He is often chosen to accompany your brother and I on hunts, and we have become quite well-acquainted."

"Oh, I myself am not particularly partial to Jackie," Emmeline responded with a small frown. "He is the alpha of the pack, you understand, and I find him quite the domineering one. While I will admit he is very charming, sir, I find my affections better spent on Thomas and Akira."

"Akira, my lady?" Captain Jamison echoed, about to ask a question, but he was interrupted by a loud bark sounding out from the side of the house. Emmeline smiled. While she avoided showing favouritism to the big black dog, she would recognise Jackie's excited bark anywhere.

The stable boy had to run with the sled dogs, his grip on their leashes tightening, as the canines bounded towards the lady they recognised as their single favourite human being. Emmeline laughed out loud at the sight of them. All the propriety in the world could not mask her affection toward her furry friends, and although she could not squat to pet them in front of a gentleman, she bent down slightly like she was bowing and extended her hands to greet them. Jackie was the first to pull free of the stable boy, almost toppling him. He ran ahead to rest his head against Emmeline's hand, and she gave him a satisfying scratch about his chin as he licked her hands thoroughly. Seeing their leader to this, all the other dogs followed suit and yanked away from the stable boy. Like the ground had been pulled out from under his feet, he fell flat on the pavement. With laughter and concern in her warm green eyes and a dozen dogs clambering for her attention, Emmeline enquired if he was all right. Mumbling that he was fine, he scrambled to his feet and retired to the stables with a slight hobble.

"They really are fond of you," Captain Jamison remarked.

"Yes," she replied, looking up to grin at him. "And this little man here"—she gave a honey brown dog a good rub on the head—"is Akira. Emmett found him on one of his trips to Japan."

"Japan?" he repeated, slight disbelief lacing his voice. "I was there with him!"

"Yes, Captain, I do believe he mentioned sailing with a friend," she concurred with a smile. "That must have been you."

"It was," he confirmed, "but I do not remember him bringing a dog back with us. In fact, I remember the captain of the ship we were on declaring animals strictly prohibited on board."

"Exactly," Emmeline replied with a wry smile.

Captain Jamison's eyes went wide with realisation. "You imply that he—?"

"Oh, Captain, we speak of Emmett Lockhart – of course he did," she answered with a laugh. She straightened and beamed at her pack of panting sled dogs. "Perhaps we should be on our way into the gardens. John? Would you be as kind as to undo their leashes for us? They're always tied up when Emmett's home, and I imagine it mustn't feel any less than absolutely horrible."

"Of course, my lady." The butler smiled kindly and complied. The dogs yipped delightfully, glad to be unshackled, but when Emmeline stepped onto the path that led to the garden and snapped her fingers, saying a gentle and almost motherly "come along, now," they were at her heel in an instant, trotting in two neat rows the way they had been trained to do pulling a sled. John and Penny walked a respectful distance away from them, careful not to accidentally listen in on the conversation between their mistress and the captain. Instead, they occupied themselves by debating the trustworthiness of the new seamstress making Lady Emmeline's dresses. She had quite a reputation, but the young lady seemed to be quite assured in doing business with her.

Captain Jamison, in the meantime, was quite astounded at the sight of Emmeline handling the sled dogs. "Why, you work so well with them."

The young lady just laughed, reaching out to caress Jackie's forehead as he walked next to her at the front of the line. "Well, I suppose sneaking them treats behind Emmett's back only helps our relationship."

An amused expression crossed the captain's face before he posed another question. "Is Emmett very strict with them?"

"Well, Captain, I suppose they are meant to be sled dogs," she answered, and for a while even she was surprised that she was defending her brother's stand on the matter. "Perhaps my spoiling them does not help them serve that function very well."

"Perhaps," he parroted with a wry smile, sarcasm well-meaning as he tried to crack a joke.

Emmeline noticed his humour and laughed. "Perhaps," she hummed again, letting her eyes sweep over the manicured garden Emmett ensured remained in perfect condition. She enjoyed spending her time outside, reading or walking or just being. The garden was one of her favourite places to spend her time, second only to the music room. She was glad Emmett kept it so well-tended.

"Has Emmett written to you at all, my lady?" Captain Jamison enquired after some time spent in comfortable silence.

"No, sir, not yet," Emmeline said. "He departed yesterday, and is only due to arrive in London at luncheon today. He couldn't have had any chance to write yet."

"I see," he replied with an easy smile. "Will you send him my best wishes should you write him soon? And let him know I called in his absence. Perhaps when I call on him next you might join us, if a hunt would interest you at all."

"Oh sir, I would be most obliged if you would permit me to intrude so," she responded, looking up at him with a grin. She had always wanted to watch a hunt up close. "I love to ride, and I can only imagine the thrill a hunt would bring."

"I am very glad to hear it," he cheered. "I wonder, my lady, if you are as skilled with horses as you are with dogs – you know, riding a horse is one thing, but hunting is another..."

***

"A LETTER FOR YOU, MY LADY, FROM LORD PORTSMOUTH." John slid the wax-sealed envelope in front of Emmeline at the dining table.

"Oh, wonderful," Emmeline said cheerily, offering the butler a smile. "Thank you, John. Do remind the stable boy to wash the dogs – they had quite a bit of fun during our walk today, and their coats are soiled. I trust they supped well?"

"They are very well, my lady. I will remind the stable boy to clean their coats," the butler replied with a courteous smile. "I will be off now. Enjoy your supper, my lady."

Emmeline thanked him again before he retreated. Once she was finally alone in the dining room with Penny, she allowed herself to tuck into the steaming plate with more gusto than was ladylike. Adalberto never failed to dazzle her with his superhuman culinary skills. Despite her talent in baking excellent blueberry pie, using a recipe her mother had devised but taught to her by the chef himself, Emmeline was able to do little else in the kitchen. She had grown up with Adalberto always on the ready to whip up a delightful meal for her, and never found the need to learn to cook. Her governess had never made her try, either. To the straight-laced governess Miss Paltrow, a true lady of status would never need to learn to cook.

Upon filling her stomach, Emmeline picked up the envelope, turning it over in her hand as she read her brother's spidery writing. To Lady Emmeline A. Lockhart. She broke open the wax seal to find a sheet of Emmett's favourite tinted letter paper. It most certainly did not come cheaply, but the young earl seemed to believe quite ardently that the material on which a letter was written made a difference in the quality of the letter. The mere thought of the fact that Emmett only used this letter paper when writing to his very dearest friends and family made Emmeline's smile stretch wider.

Dear Sister

I hope this letter finds you well. Your blueberry pie was wonderful, as always. Thank you for it – the long carriage ride was a lot more bearable with it for company.

Hardly a day spent in London and I miss you already. I intend to see to it that this letter is on its way to you immediately after I finish it because I'd like to hear from you as soon as I can. You ought to have it by suppertime tomorrow. Pray write me back as soon as you can. All this decorum will have me out of my mind by the end of the week.

You must wish to hear about Father. There is no pleasant way to describe him but that he is as he always is. You understand. I gave him your love, and he wishes me to inform you that he is in the process of finding you a suitor. For some reason staying with your brother for the rest of your life would hardly be proper...and for perhaps the same reason me living unmarried with my sister for the rest of my life seems to be equally unbecoming in his eyes. I must stress at this point, however, that I think you are the best lady my estate could have to call its own and you would live with me for all of time if I had a say in any of this.

Do inform me immediately if anything out of the ordinary happens at the house. I should like to be assured that you are well...even in my absence. You must miss me dearly.

To end... Please make sure the sled dogs get fed—and do not spoil them while I am away.

With loveEarl of Portsmouthbut more importantly...your brother always

Emmett A. Lockhart

Emmeline smiled. Emmett had always been so sweet to her. And so be it if her father was seeking her a suitor; there wasn't a chance that he would be successful anyway. Nobody in the dukedom – or, in fact, the entire kingdom – would have any desire to marry her. Years of standing alone in soirées had been enough to show her that. She didn't stand a chance at marriage – or rather, in this case, her father didn't stand a chance at marrying her off.

She folded the letter and slid it gingerly back into the caramel-coloured envelope. After she had daubed gently at her lips with her napkin, she stood and smoothed down the skirt of her peach autumn dress. In a practiced measured voice, soft like a lady's should be but loud enough to be heard and to be authoritative, she summoned Penny to her side. The duo left the room together, the lady just a step in front of her lady's maid the entire time as they navigated to the house towards Emmeline's private study.

Penny retreated into a corner as Emmeline sat in front of her desk and chose a amber-tinted sheet of letter paper and smoothed it out across her desk. Picking up her quill and dipping it in the navy blue ink she favoured, she began to compose a letter in response to her brother's.

Dear Emmett

It is lovely to hear from you so soon. All is well at home. You might like to know that Captain Peter Jamison came to visit this week, and I think you will be happy to hear that we are now friends. He came to see you, really, but like any good host would do, like YOU would do, I kept him for tea. Yesterday he called again for a walk with your sled dogs – fret not, we remained at all times within your grounds in the garden, chaperoned by John and Penny both. It was a most delightfully spent afternoon. Captain Jamison is wonderful company, and I understand why you are so fond of him yourself.

Indeed, I cannot say I am surprised to hear of Father's search for matches for us both. He should be most spoilt for choice in YOUR case, I imagine, but he shall have a difficult time with me. I think he will eventually give up – though I promise I will leave the estate once you find a new lady for it. I would hate to intrude in your life with your new wife, whomever she may be.

I wish you all the best in navigating London's peerage. I have faith in you.

I look forward to your next letter. Take care, Emmy.

BestYour sister now and forever

Emmeline A. Lockhart (Linnie)

Emmeline paused to let the ink dry, taking the time to fish out an envelope in the same colour as the letter paper from one of the dozen drawers in her desk. She folded the letter and deposited it in the envelope before writing, in her big bold penmanship, on the front:

To Right Hon. The Earl of Portsmouth E. A. Lockhart

From Lady E. A. Lockhart

She then ordered Penny to bring her the wax seal stamp, and flipping the envelope over, she branded it with her family's elaborate crest. She had always loved doing that. It made a lady with no actual function in society feel important, like she had important business that didn't concern blueberry pie.

"Have this to John," she instructed, handing her lady's maid the envelope. "Let him know that it is of utmost importance that this is delivered to my brother in the family residence in London immediately. The Earl claims he shall lose his sanity by the end of the week, and I do not intend for that to happen."

Penny smiled. "Of course, my lady."

Chapter Four

A /N THANK YOU @curlygirl78 for your three votes! You made me so happy! I'm not sure if you've seen the updated description for The Lady Lockhart, but updates will be (as far as possible) every Wednesday (or Tuesday, depending on your timezone) from now on. :)

LORD WILLIAM MAYFAIR PACED IN HIS LIBRARY. His son sat nearby and watched his parent worry relentlessly, his chin resting on the heel of his palm and his elbow supported by the arm of the chair. He had long since given up trying not to look bored.

"Your mother would know what to do if she were here," William said. "That woman knew next to nothing about high society and all its workings, and she was hardly proper, but she was good with people. She would be able to catch your sister a husband."

Emmett bristled at this blatant insult towards his mother – his father's wife – but found the strength in him to say nothing. Mother was plenty proper, he thought, she just wasn't stiff like you.

"How on earth am I to find Emmeline a match?" the duke went on to ask no one in particular. "How do women handle these things?"

"Perhaps we should ask a woman," Emmett nearly groaned as he sunk back into the plush chair, more than ready to retire to his room for the night. "Such as, perhaps, Aunt Beth?"

"How many times must I tell you this? I despise Bethany Rutherford," his father spat with viciousness most did not use when speaking of their sisters-in-law. "Her arrogance brings shame to her family name and she is foolish even for a woman. I absolutely refuse to ask her for help."

"You are being difficult, Father," Emmett replied, his tone growing clipped.

"I'm trying to secure your sister's future, Emmett; and you are not permitted to speak to your father like that."

"You called me here on urgent business, Father, but all I see is frivolity." Emmett rose, beyond tired of the situation. "I know no more than you about finding suitors for Emmeline, and you refuse to seek the help you truly need. I have suggested time and time again that we ask our closest female relation for help but you refuse to do the necessary. As such, I will be returning to Portsmouth tomorrow morning and Emmeline will remain in my care for as long as she lives unmarried, even it is forever. Good night."

"Son—" William tried to shout after the young man, but he had disappeared through the library's doors. He sighed. His boy would never understand. Brash and hot-blooded, Emmett had never paused to think. The young earl fancied himself liberal, but some would call him a rebel. Of course, it could be argued that these were just common characteristics of all young men – reckless and hungry to stand out and make change; but if Emmett was to one day be the Duke of Mayfair, it was imperative that he change his ways. He had to realise that there were many things he did not understand, things a man with a heart like his might never comprehend; things he had to learn to accept in silent compliance.

The first of these things would be marriage – namely his parents'. Lady Anne Lockhart-Rutherford was a beauty and had outstanding charm. Coupled with her social standing – she was the eldest daughter of a marquis – and the substantial dowry she had, she had been a favourable match for the young William Lockhart, then the Earl of Portsmouth. The Lockhart family was powerful, as was the Rutherford clan; and together they were invincible. The marriage was a logical decision on the part of William's pragmatic father, not a matter of the heart, for William did not love Anne; and he could never give her his everything even though the heavens above knew he had tried his hardest. Prior to his marriage, he had only ever loved one person – his mother, who did not love him back. His father had never been affectionate towards him, and he never tried to express such sentiment towards the man he only viewed as authority.

Lady Anne had always been free-spirited. She was a lady in every sense of the word, raised in the same way William had been, but cared little for many of the strict norms her society believed in. Despite everything she had been conditioned to believe, she had always sought joy from experiences instead of material comforts. When she gained knowledge of her arranged marriage, she decided that it would be a fresh start for her, a way to build her own life. She wanted little else than to live free and be happy with her new husband and the children she would bear. She tried to make her dreams a reality. She tried to love her husband but none of this was to be; for after her departure from the cage that was the Rutherford estate she remained caged by a loveless marriage governed by the strict rules her parents raised her under. Her only solaces were her two beautiful children, whom she raised to love life as passionately as she had.

After his first wife passed away due to a disease the best physicians in the dukedom could not make go away, William Lockhart had once attempted to remarry. After all, how could a man live wholly without a wife? But when he had informed his children of the whole arrangement, their faces had fallen with looks of such devastation that William had called the union off. He remembered his son's expression most vividly. The boy, only ten and seven at the time, had looked a mix of horrified and crushed, for he was under the impression that his wonderful mother would be replaced; and William Lockhart decided just one week before the wedding that he would ruin Countess Riddell's reputation before he would break his children's hearts.

The duke had never expected his son to turn and point an accusatory finger at him, claiming that he had no conscience for destroying Countess Riddell's marital prospects. His sweet daughter's crystalline emerald eyes had turned to ice when she heard her brother speak of the ruination Duke Mayfair had brought upon the noblewoman, and the next thing the duke knew, his children were on a carriage to live away from him in Portsmouth.

William said nothing of the event since then. He had never been one to display emotion openly, not even to his own flesh and blood; and he was so overjoyed when his children returned to visit him for Christmas that he decided never to speak of the incident again so as not to open old wounds.

In that moment, however, looking at the door Emmett had left to slam shut, he was not sure if those wounds had ever closed.

***

EMMETT HURLED HIS BELONGINGS INTO HIS SUITCASE WITH RAGE coursing through his veins. How dare his father insult his mother so and call his beloved aunt a disgrace? Society might have dictated that Duke Mayfair had authority over him, but Emmett had no intention to stay and waste his time away on this urgent business. Regardless of what his father thought of his change in plans, he would be cutting his two-week long trip short to a brief visit of four days. He would leave the first thing in the morn on the fifth.

"My lord," a servant called, following a knock on his door. "A letter, from the young lady, delivered at the fastest possible speed."

Emmett felt a wave of happiness wash over him, momentarily extinguishing the burning rage in his gut, and rushed to open the door. He received the letter and hastily opened it, breaking the wax seal without the caution his sister tended to take. Pulling out the letter paper, he unfolded it and began to read. His eyebrows shot up when he read of Jamison visiting with the young lady Emmeline; could the captain have intentions of courting her? No. It was all he had feared would happen. He felt a strange feeling similar to seasickness start to rock his stomach. Emmeline was his sister, Peter was like his brother, and he just could not, for the life of him, picture them together. He had worked to keep this relationship with the captain and his life with his sister discrete, and now that he was away from Portsmouth, they were melding together at a speed he was not fond of at all. He would marry her, she would go with him on all his expeditions to the various colonies, and for all his superficial friends, Emmett Lockhart would be left with no one by his side.

He folded the letter and tossed it carelessly onto his desk, collapsing onto the bed he had used throughout his adolescence. It had seemed luxuriously large back when he lived with his father, but at twenty and three and much more grown up then he had ever been, he felt it somewhat cramped. His feet dangled over the edge of the wooden frame and he sighed as he remembered the days when his mother would tuck him in, pulling his blanket up to his chin and laying a loving kiss upon his forehead like he, just a child but her child, was worth relinquishing the entire universe for. A fond ghost of a smile played on his lips as he reminisced. Lady Anne Lockhart had really been one of a kind, rarer than the small navy blue gemstone all the way from Asia that she so loved to wear upon her neck.

With the image of Peter and Emmeline burning the back of his eyes and scarring his mind, Emmett Lockhart decided that he would contact his Aunt Beth and secure Emmeline a favourable match. He told himself that he would not let her land in the same kind of miserable marriage their mother had been trapped in, that he would save his sister from his father's ignorance and cruelty. Rising from bed, he found paper and pen and began to compose a letter he thought long overdue.

***

BETHANY RUTHERFORD WAS IN THE PARLOUR OF RUTHERFORD HOUSE embroidering a pair of silk socks for her first grandchild when a servant rushed into the room, bowing deeply to greet his mistress.

"Your Ladyship," the servant said, struggling to catch his breath from all the exertion that he had put himself through to deliver the blue-tinted envelope he presently clutched in his hands, "a letter for you, my lady. Urgent business, the messenger said. Very urgent."

"Well, I certainly wasn't expecting very urgent business," Bethany said, clearing her throat as she straightened and raised her chin, nestling deeper into her cushioned velvet sofa with gold inlay on the polished wooden frame. It had become her favourite seat in the parlour ever since her husband had forked out a small fortune to purchase it for her. "Let me have it, then, boy."

The servant obliged and excused himself before scurrying out of the room.

She spied the familiar wax seal and wondered what on earth the irksome William Lockhart might want to do with her; but then she read the fine hand on the front of the envelope and realised it must be her beloved nephew writing her this fine day. With that thought in mind, a loving smile rarely seen on Bethany Rutherford's face surfaced as she daintily opened the letter.

Dear Aunt Bethany

I hope this letter finds you in the pink of health.

It must have been at least a decade since I last saw you. Truly – I am deeply apologetic for my lack of correspondence. I beseech you understand that I have many new duties to attend to in Portsmouth now, and seek your forgiveness on my failure to write you. Today I am in my father's estate in London and write to you in need of a favour.

Bethany's eyebrows raised in pleasant surprise. It was true. The last time she had seen darling Emmett he was but a boy, the last she had heard from him he was but eighteen and relocating to Portsmouth with her dear, sweet niece, and now he must be...twenty and three. And what a tactful young lord he has grown into; his letter was honey sweet. "How time flies," she tutted under her breath before resuming her perusal of the letter with a contented smile upon her aged face.

My dearest sister Emmeline is in need of a husband. She is twenty and three, you understand, as I am, and is very much of age to be married. It is quite unfortunate that she has been unsuccessful in securing a proposal thus far although she has attended quite a number of soirées in the past. Father wishes to marry her off but is not equipped with the proper knowledge regarding how a good match should be acquired for her, and I fear that if he is left to his own devices he will land my poor sister a lifetime as unhappy as Mother's was.

Seeing as you are my closest female relation I think it most apt that I turn to you for help.—Bethany's heart swelled with pride at this juncture, for yes, she was his aunt, the only aunt of such a wonderful young earl, and he needed her.—Father will not request your assistance, but for Emmeline's sake I shall ask you myself.

Thank you very much, Aunt Beth; you have my love, and Emmeline's.

Yours faithfullyYour nephewEmmett L.

Bethany grinned as she realised what her receiving this letter entailed; she would be in charge of Emmeline's marital affairs! She, blessed with three sons, had never had a daughter to find a husband and arrange a wedding for, but now she had the chance to do what every woman dreamed of. She would do a splendid job of marrying her niece off. Even if she did not love Emmeline enough to do so of her own accord – which she most certainly did–, she owed it to Anne, her favourite sister since the beginning, to secure the sweet young lady a future worthy of her pure heart. Now that the girl's own mother was deceased, she would take on the responsibilities poor Anne had left behind and ensure that her niece lived the best future she possibly could. She would not stand for anything else.

"Well," Bethany huffed, standing hurriedly. "I must begin immediately. Any happiness in life Emmeline is to have depends on me now – me!"

Then a sudden thought struck her with great force and she almost fell back into her sofa. Why, she should have thought of this instantly when she first read her nephew's letter!

She smiled gleefully. She knew of just the right person for her precious Emmeline.

***

THE LETTER SAT IN THE PILE OF MAIL ATOP A SILVER PLAT-TER, BALANCED on the steady hand of a servant as he strode through the hallways. When he had arrived at his first destination, he slipped through the service door and laid the wax-sealed envelope atop a small table in the study.

An hour later she returned from her tea. She saw the familiar hand on the front of the envelope and smiled. She remembered it quite fondly. Bethany Rutherford had not been pleasant to all; but the pompous daughter of a marquis had made an exception and been so kind to her. Her, who then, had not been who she later became.

Your Majesty

It is I, your old friend Bethany Rutherford. We attended finishing school together. You must be awfully busy with your queenly duties in the palace but I feel like I would be doing the nation a disservice if I did not inform you of this news promptly.

I have heard of His Highness Crown Prince Alexander's search for a wife; and there is one lady I think would suit Prince Alexander splendidly. I would, most sincerely and wholeheartedly, suggest my niece, Lady Emmeline Lockhart. First and foremost, she is of similar age to His Highness; I do believe she is only one year younger. More importantly, however, Emmeline is the daughter of the Duke of Mayfair (no doubt, strengthening your ties with Mayfair would be exceedingly advantageous for the royal family) and very popular with the people of Portsmouth, where she lives with her brother the Earl. It is also noteworthy that her brother Lord Lockhart has excellent ties with many other members of the peerage due to his generosity and would be a very good ally to have. For stronger ties with him would signify stronger ties with virtually all noblemen.

Emmeline is also, of course, perfect as a successor for you. She was raised by the strictest of all governesses in the dukedom Madam Helena Paltrow and is wonderfully refined. She plays the pianoforte well and is also skilled in needlework. She is well-known in Portsmouth for her kindness and charity.

She is very literate, schooled in the refined languages and especially fluent in Italian and French, and outstandingly intelligent – an immensely desirable quality, I imagine, for a queen.

As such, Your Majesty, I would highly recommend Lady Emmeline Lockhart of Portsmouth as one of the ladies considered for His Highness's wedding. If His Highness Prince Alexander should take a liking to her, she would be a most advantageous match for him. Having her as a part of the royal family would lend you a lot more political traction.

I anticipate favourable news. You have my thanks in advance.

Yours sincerelyBethany F. Rutherford

Chapter Five

- -

A/N

Hi there! Exciting news – The Lady Lockhart has reached #683 on Historical Fiction as of 24 September, 2016! Thank you so much for all your support! I can hardly believe this! To celebrate, here's Chapter Five ahead of time.

That said, I would really really love to get more feedback. I often find myself thinking of how to make this a better reading experience for you and not having a clue about what I should do. Here's my proposition: if you guys could give me three feedback on TLL before this Wednesday, I'll be publishing Chapter Six ahead of time (again! YAS for early updates!). Chapter Five is actually very short in terms of word count, and I thought another early update would be nice.

So without further ado, here's Chapter Five (exceedingly short, like I mentioned - sorry). I can't wait to hear from you!

x L

LADY EMMELINE ARTEMIS LOCKHARTyou are cordially invited toTEA WITH HER MAJESTY QUEEN SARAH THE FIRST at

ST JAMES'S PALACE NEXT FRIDAY AFTERNOON.

ACCOMMODATION WILL BE PROVIDED SHOULD YOU RE-QUIRE IT.YOU MAY BRING YOUR OWN MAIDS-IN-WAITING. HOWEVER, HER MAJESTY WOULD BE MOST GLAD TO SUP-PLY YOU WITH TWO SHOULD YOU BE UNABLE TO DO SO.H ER MAJESTY QUEEN SARAH LOOKS FORWARD TO MEETING YOU.

*Update: We just dropped to #950! Do vote and comment to pull us back up!

Chapter Six

A/N Hello again! Here's your weekly update! But before that, three things to address in today's Author's Note:

1: Dedication - this chapter is dedicated to the ever-lovely @curlygirl78. Thank you so much for all your support! We're up to #738 in Historical Fiction - hooray!

2: Comments - For this chapter, let me know if you'd like me to make my author's notes shorter or longer, and if you want them at the start or end of chapters.

3: Update Schedule / Timezones - I just realised today that my schedule might be confusing for some of you. As I live in the southern hemisphere, I update every Wednesday during the daytime in my timezone; but some of you may receive updates in the dead of the night on Tuesday (depending of course on where you live). I hope this clears any potential doubt up. :)

That's all for now; enjoy the chapter!

"TO LONDON FOR TEA, MY LADY?" PENNY LOOKED POSITIVELY BAFFLED. Her mistress had been most enigmatic in her explanations of her trip. Why would anyone make the trip to London for tea?

"Yes," Emmeline replied as she pulled another armful of dresses out of her closet before turning to smile wryly at her maid. "To London for tea with Her Majesty Queen Sarah, and we then shall stay briefly with my father before returning to Portsmouth with my brother."

"The Queen," Penny echoed, nearly swooning. "The Queen?"

Emmeline laughed, handing the garments to the awestruck girl. "Yes; the Queen. Truly, Penny, it took me three whole days to comprehend that the invitation was not a figment of my imagination. I do wonder what Her Majesty would want to do with me."

"Perhaps it's to do with His Grace your father," Penny suggested as she proceeded to pack the dresses into a suitcase.

"Why would she ask me to tea then?" Emmeline cast her lady's maid a quizzical look across the room.

Unable to answer this question, the servant just shrugged as she bent down to fit everything in nicely. "I know far less of these matters than you, my lady."

"Well," Emmeline sighed, "I'm just glad we started using your mother's miracle oils last week. My hair is much more suited to meet Her Majesty now – you must convey my sincerest thanks to Mrs Smith the next time you see her."

"As I said, my lady, you have beautiful hair by nature." Penny smiled. "Thick hair tends to require more care than usual."

Her mistress only offered her a smile in reply.

"I think we've packed everything I need," Emmeline declared, clapping her hands together. "We've prepared my dresses and my jewellery, and my creams and powders as well as my book. I don't imagine I'd need anything else – after all, we will be staying with Father. What of your luggage, Penny? Is it ready?"

"Yes, my lady, I prepared my things last week after you mentioned that we'd be going on a trip," she answered with an smile. "If I may speak my mind, my lady, I'm wonderfully excited. I've never been to London."

Emmeline frowned. "I don't particularly fancy the city, but I hear the palace is beautiful. The duke's property, Wellington House, is pleasant to look at as well; far larger than this estate, for certain." She paused. "I, however, do not look forward to seeing Father again."

Penny grimaced. "I'm sorry, my lady. Please, I did not mean to upset you."

"No, no," the young lady dismissed her concerns, waving them off with a flippant hand. Then her eyes brightened as a new topic formed in her mind, and she thought of a particularly strapping young gentleman she had grown to love daydreaming about like the lovesick girl she absolutely was not.

"I've had this on my mind for a while, now, Penny, and I would very much appreciate your input – how do I express this? Say, do you think Captain Jamison... Well, do you think he fancies me? It's not that I—Only, in the past week he called on me for tea three times even though I have explicitly informed him that Emmett is not home."

"The captain? Why, my lady," she replied, sporting a grin the Cheshire Cat would have been proud of. "I have maintained silence about this matter since it does not seem to be any of my business, but if you truly wish to have my humble opinion, I think he most certainly does. Frequent calling aside, I think he looks at you in a very special way. There is a warmth in his eyes, my lady, and if I did not know better perhaps I might even think the pair of you engaged."

"Truly?" Emmeline almost swooned. "Oh!"

"You take a fancy to him yourself, do you not, my lady?"

The lady turned a deep shade of scarlet and very decidedly turned away from the teasing young maid, saying nothing else on the matter. This to Penny was a very clear yes, and she giggled, drawing a small smile she did not see.

***

"HOW WAS THE RIDE, SISTER?" EMMETT ASKED AS HE AS-SISTED HIS TWIN in disembarking the carriage.

"Uneventful," she replied with a smile. He kissed her knuckles in the customary greeting and she bobbed a quick curtsy. "Thank you for coming to greet us. Truly, I have missed you."

"As I you," the earl replied with a grin. "I trust Peter knows Lockhart Manor will be empty for the next week or two?"

"Yes," Emmeline answered, accepting the arm he offered her as they began the hike up the stairs leading to the main door of Wellington House from the driveway. "I wrote him about our trip. He has mentioned calling again when we are both home."

"Very good," her brother said as they approached the main door of the house. "I wrote him as well, but have not heard back. I do suppose the distance my letter must travel to reach him has to do with it."

"Of course it has, why would you think otherwise?" she responded; then, with a teasing smirk, "Why, has being away from Portsmouth turned you into a fool already?"

He shook his head, but chuckled quietly to himself. "You will never learn to curb your sharp tongue."

"What can I say?" she laughed, "It lends me character."

They reached the top of the stairs, and a footman held the large oak doors open for them. "His Grace expects you in the drawing room, my lord."

Emmett offered a curt nod in reply and guided his sister through the familiar halls they had spent their childhoods frolicking in until at last they arrived in front of the drawing room that their mother had once poured her heart and soul into decorating. Upon entering it, Emmeline was disappointed to find it drab and lifeless, nothing like the vibrant Lady Anne had left it when she left the world. The curtains were the same but not the pure white they had been once upon a time – now they hung yellowed and miserable. None of the ornamental lamps her mother had taken hours to decide where to strategically place were turned on. Even the polished wooden floor looked like it was still mourning the loss of its mistress.

"Ah, children," William greeted, his voice as impersonal as ever, almost disdainful even this time. "It is... It is lovely to see you after so long, my dearest Emmeline. I trust you have been well?"

She mustered a smile for him and curtsied as low as her legs would allow her to go, knowing people like him appreciated pretentious courtesies such as these. "Good afternoon, Father. I have fared excellently. Emmett takes such wonderful care of me."

"I should hope so," he replied, his deep, authoritative voice grave as always even as he spoke of nothing particularly serious. "You are aware that I am seeking you a match?"

"Yes – I am aware that you are trying to do so," she replied, the sarcasm clear in her words.

William Lockhart did not flinch. "Good. I would like you to be honest with me now; you must speak at once if there is any gentleman you already...take a fancy to." He paused and paced to the large window that took up the entirety of one wall in the room before lingering there, gazing upon his massive estate. "Now, Emmeline, I know you think me unfamiliar with the workings of arranging a match for my daughter, but I should not like to cage—I should not like to have you in...in a marriage that is...unwilling. You know your mother—" Something snagged in his throat, but he simply cleared it like it was nothing and continued. "Your mother would never forgive me if I did."

"There is no one," Emmett replied. "At least, not that I know of. Emmeline?"

She gazed upon her brother. Captain Peter Jamison, she wanted to announce; but for now Captain Jamison likely considered her as no less than a friend – for she herself had snubbed his romantic advance –, and when she thought of what her brother might feel about her fancying the one man he had once so explicitly told her not to take interest in, the idea of wishing to confess her possible match with the captain fled entirely and she swallowed the words already at her throat.

"No, Father," she heard herself saying instead. "None yet."

"Very well," William said, sighing almost as if he regretted her answer. "However, Emmeline, remember this: if you are, one day in the near future, to find a gentleman you fancy outside of my and your brother's choosing, you may inform me of it. I will do everything within my power to secure you a desirable union."

"Thank you," she said with all the clipped politeness a lady should use on those she dislikes, and inwardly she scoffed at his words. Would he really do as he promised? It was unlikely: he was, after all, a man without a heart and without a soul. He did not love his wife; he did not love his fiancée; he never showed any love for his children. He had already ruined the lives of two women. Who was to say that she, the only one left in his life to destroy, would not be the third?

"I will excuse you now, Emmeline," he announced. "I have to speak with your brother about his marital prospects. I will send a maid to call you down for tea. Your appointment at the palace is come Friday, correct?"

"Yes," Emmeline replied before curtsying once again. "I shall see you at tea. Emmett." With that, she swept out of the room to find Penny awaiting her by the door of the drawing room along with a footman she vaguely recognised.

Emmeline was shown to her room and left with Penny to settle in. The maid immediately started unpacking Emmeline's things, arranging her dresses in the cupboard, placing her jewellery neatly in drawers in the vanity. She set the bottle of oil for Emmeline's hair in the adjacent bathroom, along with the powders and creams Emmeline would need to make herself up for her meeting with the Queen. The young lady was not used to wearing anything on her face, but for this special appointment she felt obliged to look her prettiest. After all, it could be the only chance she would ever have to sit down with the Queen of England for tea.

"I wonder how Father intends to find Emmett a wife," Emmeline said after some period of time. "I imagine he shall be spoilt for choice... How does one pick a single deserving woman out of so many?"

"If I may, my lady," Penny, who was standing beside her, answered, "I think love always finds a way. A woman kan Lord Lockhart deserves will be one deserving of the title Countess."

"I should hope so," she replied. "I think there is not a single soul that should have happiness more than my brother. You know how good he is to me..."

***

"WHAT ABOUT YOU, SON?" WILLIAM ASKED THE MOMENT
PENNY CLOSED the door behind her, as he took a seat in the sofa that
the family had always been silently considered his. "Have you any lady I
should know of?"

"No," Emmett said stonily. "You are aware of this. I do not intend to marry."

"Nonsense," he responded with a dismissive wave of his hand. "The Lockhart family needs an heir to my estate, what will someday be yours. Besi
des...being married is an important part of life, and I promised... Emmett,
what do you think of a Marquis's daughter?"

"A Marquis's daughter – like Mama, you mean? A favourable match?"

"Emmett, your mother and I—"

"As I have informed you multiple times, Father, I do not intend to marry,"
the young earl spat through gritted teeth, not deigning to notice that he
had interrupted his father. Politeness had long ceased to exist between
father and son.

His brow crumpled. "I do not understand your stubbornness. What is it
about matrimony that repulses you so?"

"I never want to hurt a woman the way you did." Emmett turned away,
thrusting his chin up like an impetuous child standing up to his father, the
child he had once been – and, perhaps, in some ways, still was.

"And yet you engage Bethany Rutherford's help to marry Emmeline off to
a prince, so that your sister, whom you claim to love, might be hurt in that
fashion?"

"I do not intend for Emmeline to be hurt in any fashion," the younger Lockhart replied, the volume of his voice rising slightly. "And you will not imply that I do not love her. I love her more than anything, and even if I did not care for her so, you have been far from dutiful—"

"Oh, I imply nothing of the sort," William replied. "In fact, I think no one has ever shown her more affection than you have, and I thank you – sincerely – for it. I only imply that you do not love her more than you love yourself."

"Excuse me?" Emmett demanded, whirling back around to face his father, his fists shaking. "What is the meaning of that supposed to be? Are you now accusing me of being as callous and unfeeling as you, saying that I would ruin my own sister in a bid to make some good connections, after I witnessed you murder my mother for the same reason?"

"Emmett, you know your mother died of illness." There was an odd tenderness in William's typically brusque voice.

"She only ever got sick because you upset her so!" Emmett argued fiercely.

"Emmett..." William made as if to answer his remark, but stopped and paid no further attention to the matter, instead merely rising from his chair with a long sigh. "I will look into inviting Lady Adelaide Farthingale and her father Lord Coppershire to Wellington House for a meal. If she takes to you well and you decide that you fancy her in return, I will speak to him about your union."

The Duke of Mayfair offered his son a curt nod and stalked out of the room, leaving Emmett standing and staring after his retreating figure, seething with indignation.

"How dare you!" he roared to an open door, his entire body shaking with ire. Yet there was nothing much he could ever really do about William – he was, after all, his father.

Meanwhile, hearing his child shout at him so over the thud of his footsteps William's heart was as heavy as his gait. Yet there was nothing much he could ever really do about Emmett – he was, after all, his son.

Chapter Seven

Happy late Tuesday! Early update this week! I wanted to wait till tomorrow to publish this on the scheduled day, but I have exciting news in the Author's Note and I couldn't wait any longer!

"OH, AUNT BETH!" EMMELINE CRIED, RUSHING DOWN THE HALL INTO THE drawing room to greet the extravagantly-dressed lady who had just arrived at Wellington House. Emmett was out of the house meeting with a lord he was familiar with who was passing through London, and William had refused to welcome Bethany into his home. Thus, the duty of receiving the guest fell upon Emmeline's small shoulders – but, as a trained lady, greeting her aunt was nothing she could not handle. "I have missed you so!"

"As I have missed you, my darling," Bethany crooned, smiling with pleasure as she watched her niece drop into a low curtsy like the refined lady she was always destined to be. After Emmeline had risen, Bethany drew her into her arms for a tight embrace. "My, what a lovely thing you have grown into. Just look at you!"

"Oh, Aunt Beth, thank you for your kind words, but I am far from lovely," Emmeline responded with a strained laugh.

Bethany's brow furrowed immediately. "Emmeline, darling, you are the loveliest young lady I have ever known. Do not let anyone tell you otherwise."

Emmeline shook her head vehemently at this statement, but decided to change the subject instead of dwelling on her lack of physical beauty. It was, understandably, something she did not enjoy debating. "Come, Aunt, do let me show you to one of the guest rooms. Penelope, carry her luggage, will you?"

Penny complied silently, knowing that she should behave differently before the likes of Bethany Rutherford from when she was alone with her mistress. Bethany linked arms with Emmeline as they began towards one of the house's finer guest suites, chattering about the newest renovations in Rutherford House's parlour. She was not terribly interested in the new detailing on the ceiling, but listened politely, occasionally offering words of approval and appreciation as a lady should do in that situation.

"Here it is, Aunt," Emmeline announced when they arrived in front of a large door with gold inlay in the doorframe. "The finest room Wellington House has to offer. Do let me know if you require anything else, and I will see to it that your needs are met."

Bethany held her niece by the arms and beamed affectionately at her. "You have beautiful manners, my darling – a true lady indeed."

Emmeline managed a laugh. "Thank you, Aunt Bethany, but I think I do not deserve such praise. This is the least I can do for you. Ring the bell if you need anything at all. We will have tea in an hour or so – I will send a maid to escort you to the dining room."

She bobbed a curtsy and left her aunt to rest, shutting the door and heading back to her room with Penny in tow. When they were a safe distance away, she turned to the other girl and asked, "Tell me, Penny – what do you think of my aunt Bethany?"

"I think she loves you very much, my lady," the maid in waiting answered. "She seems to think the world of you, and in my humble opinion, I think she is not at all wrong in doing so. What she says is true – my lady, shall you ever realise that you are beyond conventional beauty?"

Emmeline produced a noncommittal hum.

Knowingly, Penny said nothing else.

***

EMMELINE MISSED ADALBERTO'S COOKING, BUT SAID NOTHING, INSTEAD nibbling on a rather tasteless biscuit in courteous silence as Bethany chattered on and on about her own days in finishing school. Her niece wished more than anything in that moment that her stories were interesting. Unfortunately, however, Emmeline had, over many years, found that most of her wishes did not come true. "My mother – your grandmother – sent me to the finest finishing school in all of London. She sent all of us, you know, even your silly Aunt Caitlyn, and of course your mother attended the same school. If memory still serves me well, however, she did not like it very much..."

Bethany never did pick up on her boredom, and talked about each and every girl she knew from finishing school – none of whom she liked – for at least an hour more before she said something that made the sleepy young lady sit quite a great deal straighter in her chair.

"Anyway, the point of this story is, everyone was horrible except for this one girl I knew back then... Her name was – is – Sarah. I believe she sent you an invitation to tea this Friday?"

"What, you speak of Her Majesty Queen Sarah?" Emmeline exclaimed.

She laughed. "Well, yes, my darling. Her Majesty Queen Sarah – but she was only Miss Sarah Canterbury back then, not even a member of the peerage, just a merchant's daughter. Understandably, she was not very popular with all those horrid girls, but she and I were like old friends perhaps the moment we met. I like to think that people who are truly noble have a connection, you know, and those other brats were definitely far from good enough to be true nobility. As for Sarah…well, she is Queen now, and I think that speaks volumes about her status."

"I think so very highly of Her Majesty," the younger woman could not help but declare. "She is so poised and so remarkably learned, and I think every woman in the world should strive to be like her. And I am to have tea with her come Friday! Oh, Aunt Beth, what if I make her detest me?"

Bethany smiled lovingly at her niece. "If I may say so myself, darling Emmeline, I think you are quite poised and learned yourself. Knowing Sarah, I am quite certain that she will be rather fond of you."

"Truly?" Emmeline very nearly swooned. "Her Majesty? Fond of me?"

"Why, of course," Bethany replied. "I did, after all, write her about you."

"Is that why I've been asked to tea?" she asked, confusion in her eyes. "You wrote Her Majesty about me?"

"Well, yes," her aunt said slowly. "Yes, that is correct. I told her about how splendid you are, and—"

"Please, Aunt Beth, I fail to understand. Why would you do such a thing? What about me would be of interest to Her Majesty?" A sense of foreboding caused Emmeline's heart to hammer quite violently in her chest, and her breaths grew shallow. Yet something innate prompted her to seek clarification. She needed to know that she was not just scaring herself.

"Well, your brother wrote me seeking help to catch you a husband, my darling Emmeline, and I am sure you know that His Highness Prince Alexander is seeking a wife?"

Emmeline did swoon after all that time, well and good, her eyes rolling back in her head as she emitted a small whimper before her body fell limp in her chair.

***

WHEN SHE FINALLY CAME TO AFTER A FEW HOURS, A DAMP CLOTH WAS being daubed gingerly against her forehead. She stirred, groaning audibly as her head throbbed painfully and every fibre in her body begged for rest.

"Oh, my lady, you're awake!" Penny's voice rang out in her ears, far too loud and clear for her liking then. "Her Ladyship, someone call for Her Ladyship—"

"Cease that racket instantly," Emmeline scolded, but there was no harshness in her tone to be found. "I have a most dreadful headache and you are exacerbating it quite cruelly, Penelope."

"Oh! My apologies, my lady," Penny whispered, much to her mistress's relief. "Would you like me to fetch Her Ladyship your aunt? She instructed me to notify her the very moment you came to, but I thought you might like to...rest before I call for her."

"No, no, Penny, do not seek her now." Though she kept her eyes shut, Emmeline waved a hand reflexively in the fashion she always did when turning down one of Penny's suggestions. "You know me well. I would indeed like a few moments to myself."

"Would you like me to leave you, my lady?"

"That would not be necessary, unless you would like to rest awhile – in which case you may retire to your quarters for an hour."

"Never."

Emmeline cracked a smile at that, but said nothing more. Her maid in waiting found a seat in a chair probably meant for the household's wait staff in the far corner of the room, and occupied herself by staring out the window at William Lockhart's overgrown garden as the young lady drifted off to a peaceful sleep.

Penny somehow found entertainment from observing the sky change colour for over an hour. The young girl had always been quite fond of the boundless blue expanse above her – the sky was ever-present, one of the constants in her life, always there for her to marvel over when there was nothing else to be happy about. When she was a little girl playing in the fields of a small town she hardly remembered, the sky was like a guardian angel, a blanket over her shoulders, and she basked in its glory without understanding what exactly it was. When her father left and her mother struggled to find employment and food, she spent the evening meal feeding off the magnificence of dusk. When she first came to Wellington House seeking a job as a lowly maid, she had looked up at the large house and once again beheld the sky, telling herself over and over again that if she could still see the same sky as the one she saw at home then she must not be so far away.

And so it was with immense fondness that Penny once again gazed upon the sky, the endless ceiling that must have touched the Lord Himself. It had been a long time since she last needed to seek strength from it, but it did not feel estranged to her. For Penelope, the sky still held all the warmth of a childhood best friend.

When her mistress woke again, a glance at the time indicated that it was almost time for dinner, and she helped her bathe and dress to see her aunt again. William had sent instructions for his meal to be taken directly to his room, clearly in no mood to see Bethany anytime in the foreseeable future.

"I do apologise for collapsing earlier at tea," Emmeline told Bethany when she saw her aunt as she entered the dining room for the evening meal. "It was most improper of me."

"You were in shock, my darling; your reaction was quite understandable. After all, you will be marrying the Crown Prince of our wonderful country – I know it is a lot to take in," her aunt responded, smiling kindly at her beloved niece. "I am just glad that you are well again. I was quite worried for your wellbeing."

"Well, I assure you that you have no cause to worry any longer," she assured her aunt. Yet even as she did so, her own stomach churned with anxiety and there seemed to be something caught in her throat. "I must clarify one thing with you, Aunt Beth. You just said that I will be marrying Prince Alexander...how can you sound so certain of it?"

"Why, of course I can. Do you not remember me telling you that I wrote to the Queen recommending you for the place of future queen? Since Sarah and I are old friends, I am quite certain you will eventually be chosen to be his bride," Bethany said, her eyes lighting up and the smile on her face stretching in delight at the image of her niece being crowned queen. Yet her expression fell slightly as she detected the apprehension in Emmeline's trembling voice. "Surely you have no protest, darling?"

But the young lady was no longer listening to her aunt, and made no answer. You will be marrying the Crown Prince. You will be marrying the Crown Prince... Bethany's words reverberated endlessly in her mind. I am quite certain you will eventually be chosen to be his bride...

She longed to weep. What about Captain Jamison? she longed to cry out. He is so good to me, and I could grow to love him as he might grow to love me only given time... But now I am doomed to marry a prince? How shall I ever explain this to him?

Normally, she would have stayed silent about the captain. It was never in her nature to voice her opinions to authority – her life had never been her own, and it had long been taught to her that it would never be hers until she was a married woman. Only then would she have some agency to speak of, but even so, her husband would own her soul.

But something had to be said at that very moment, or she would be married off and caged in the palace before she could even call Peter's name.

"Aunt," she began slowly, somehow finding the courage to finally speak up about Captain Jamison although she had none, "There is a man—"

"A man? Is he courting you?" Bethany interrupted, arching an eyebrow sharply. This man, she thought, would ruin all her great plans for her niece – he stood in the way of Emmeline's lifetime of luxury, and for this reason alone she was disinclined to like him at all.

She knew, however, that it was not too late. If Emmeline did not quite love this man yet, then she could be stopped from developing further affections and subsequently made to care for Prince Alexander instead. To Bethany it was that simple.

"He has not declared that he is, but I think he might soon," Emmeline replied, fidgeting in her seat. She saw right through her aunt's intentions, and she knew that she had already lost the battle; but she still felt some obligation to try to fight it anyway. "He has called on me twice, and as of now we call each other friends."

"Do you love this man?"

"I am quite fond of him—"

"But you do not love him yet?"

Emmeline could not find it in herself to lie to her aunt.

"... No."

"Then I see no problem," Bethany announced. "You may find yourself quite fond of Prince Alexander as well. You must trust me, my darling – he is devastatingly handsome, and I daresay thrice as good as your man could ever be."

***

CAPTAIN PETER JAMISON WAS TRULY OF THE OPINION THAT HE MIGHT, well and proper, lose his mind. The letter had been sitting on his desk for days now, but he did not know how to respond to such a cruel message.

Emmeline Lockhart was a beautiful girl – more than she would ever realise. He yearned not to own but only to know her spirit, her laugh, the twinkle in her knowing green eyes. He craved for her in the least physical way a man could want a woman. He thought that he might love her already, although he never imagined it was possible to begin to care so deeply for any individual so quickly...

And yet every time he thought of her he thought of that dreaded letter, and his heart ached all over again. He was but a navy-man, not born into the peerage like Emmett was. He was no politician, while Emmett dealt with politics for a living. How could he outsmart the earl when it came to this?

He had considered disregarding his friend's cautionary message, thought of packing a suitcase, sailing straight for London, and asking Emmeline's father for her hand in marriage. Yet every time he closed his eyes he saw that letter again, every word burned into his eyes.

Dear Peter

Emmeline wrote me about your calling on her. I thought you would understand that I see you as a brother and, to me, it would hardly be acceptable for you to court her... But I see now that this, however unpleasant, must be stated explicitly. I will apologise for this, but boundaries must be drawn. I will NOT have you courting my sister for as long as you are my friend... And I beseech you take into account the fact that we have been like brothers for more than a decade.

With your position, I am more than certain you will be able to find a beautiful woman of your choice to marry. I will be able to obtain you opportunities to attend a few dances and seek a better match if you will promise to keep your distance from Emmeline.

I love her deeply and I care for you just as much. Some things are not meant to be and I will stop such things from happening – whatever it takes. Do not force my hand, Peter.

I trust you will deal with this matter sensibly... After all, you have always been a rational creature, a trait I have always admired greatly.

Thank you, brother, for your understanding in advance.

YoursEmmett

A/N Hi, everyone! I hope you enjoyed the chapter! :)

1: Updates - From next week onwards, updates will be every Friday instead of Wednesday. If there is any protest though, do feel free to leave a comment!

2: Updates, again - Due to some travelling I'll be doing, I may not be able to access Wattpad for the next eight weeks (I'm leaving town next Friday). Therefore, I have engaged the help of a friend. If possible, I will be updating TLL myself, although I will offer my apologies in advance for any potential hiccups in formatting or punctuality.

3: Comment - I'm considering changing the book title to Artemis (Emmeline's middle name). It also ties in with the plot nicely, as you will later find out. Thoughts? You can see the new cover in the Media section! :) If I get three comments about this before Chapter Eight is due, there'll be an early update as a thank-you! :)

Vote, comment, and follow! It's a little effort but it means so much :)

x Leanne

p.s. We're at #378 in Historical Fiction as of 3/10/16! This is absolutely unreal! Thank you guys SO much!

Chapter Eight - Part One

Surprise thank-you update! #251 in Historical Fiction (on 5/10/16)?! This is nuts! Thank you thank you thank you a million times over! :DD Enjoy this half of the chapter!

* Update: We've dropped back to #325 as of today (7/10/16), but that's okay! It's so humbling to even be on the What's Hot list, and it's all because of every single one of you who reads this. Thank you!

"WELCOME TO ST JAMES'S PALACE, LADY EMMELINE," THE FOOTMAN WHO helped her off the carriage greeted stonily. "Her Majesty is waiting for you in one of the drawing rooms...Greta here will take you there."

"Thank you, sir," Emmeline responded with a smile. The impassive footman offered a curt nod, and a slightly aged female servant standing by him bobbed a small curtsy. After nodding smilingly in return, Emmeline followed her into the palace with Penny right beside her, and Greta led her expertly through the halls. Each step they took provided them with a spectacular new view, and Emmeline walked through the corridors marvelling over the splendour and grandiose of the architecture and décor.

"The palace is breathtaking, Madam Greta," Emmeline remarked about halfway through the journey.

"Oh, yes, it is indeed," Greta replied with a kind smile cast briefly towards her before she focused on weaving through the twisting hallways again. "Although I must correct you, my lady – I am no Madam, only Greta."

"Well, Greta, you must feel wonderfully blessed to live here, surrounded by such beauty every day."

The servant grinned, her eyes crinkling as she turned to look briefly at Emmeline. "Aye, my lady, that I do. I have lived here for nearly forty years now, and the palace still takes my breath away every day."

"Oh, you are lucky then! I live in Portsmouth with my brother, you see, and I have only ever been to the palace once before now," she said. "I quite envy you."

"You say you envy me, my lady?" Greta chuckled. "I am but a lowly servant."

"Oh, Greta, pray do not say so!" Emmeline exclaimed, her eyes growing wide with horror at her statement. "You are hardly lowly. I admire you so! I could never know the halls of this gargantuan palace, and yet you have them memorised. You serve His Majesty, serve your country every day of your life, while I can serve no one but myself cooped up in Lockhart Manor! Between you and I, I consider you the greater nobility!"

"Yes – you must know that my mistress is so respectful of those who serve, Madam Greta," Penny quipped, her words tumbling out of her mouth faster than her feet struck the marble flooring with every step she took. "Our chef Adalberto is family to her and she treats me so wonderfully... You must never feel lowly in her presence!"

"Well... Thank you then, my lady," Greta responded, before slowing to a stop before a large door. "I have learnt much from our conversation. Her

Majesty Queen Sarah is in this room." She sunk into the lowest curtsy she could manage. "Till we meet again."

Regardless of what the others in the corridor might think about her gesture, Emmeline decided to curtsy in return. As she lifted her skirts and sank low, Penny hurriedly dropped a curtsy as well. The trio rose together, and Greta beamed at the young lady before disappearing down the hall.

"What a lovely woman," Emmeline observed with a light sigh once she was gone from their line of sight. "Truly, Penelope, it pained me to hear her speak ill of herself so."

Penny giggled. "Perhaps now you know how I feel about you, my lady?"

Emmeline beheld her maid in waiting for a moment with eyebrows furrowed in thought; but then she said nothing, instead raising her fist, drawing a long calming breath, and rapping on the drawing room door.

"Come in." The voice that called out in response was warmer than Emmeline had imagined.

Emmeline pushed the door open and entered, Penny close on her heels. Then they beheld the Queen herself, seated, in the flesh, on a royal blue sofa. Emmeline felt the blood drain from her face at the sight as if she suddenly realised that she was face to face with the monarch, and both she and her maid in waiting dropped to the lowest curtsies they had ever managed in their lives. Emmeline was so close to the floor that she could almost feel the cool marble against her skin. Her muscles screamed in protest, but she only held her position firmly, as if she was clinging on for dear life itself, and prayed that Queen Sarah could not see her shaking.

"Rise," the Queen said, and the two straightened. "Lady Emmeline Lockhart of Portsmouth, I have heard much about you."

"Your Majesty...it is a great honour to meet you." She struggled to keep the tremor out of her voice.

Queen Sarah smiled, and her eyes held only benevolence. "Come, Lady Emmeline, have a seat."

"Th-Thank you, Your Majesty." Emmeline complied and took a seat upon a sofa opposite the Queen.

"Oh, you are incredibly well-mannered, but pray do not call me that, my dear; it makes feel so terribly old!" Queen Sarah laughed good-naturedly. "You may call me Sarah. I like to think the crown atop my head does not render me above being addressed by the name I was born with. Do you not agree?"

"Oh, yes, I do agree with you," Emmeline replied with an enthusiastic nod, feeling her anxiety slowly begin to melt away at the monarch's friendliness. "I have always wondered if I—you see, Your Majesty, I do not know if it would be appropriate for me to—How do I explain this? People would talk, and—"

The queen only laughed again. "Truly, Lady Emmeline, you are every bit as endearing as your aunt said you to be. But you may address me as Sarah, and if you would be so inclined, I would like to call you Emmeline in return."

"Of course, Your—Sarah," Emmeline responded. "May I ask a question?"

"Yes, my dear?"

"Do your servants address you as Sarah also?"

"Well," Sarah sighed, "no. As you rightly pointed out yourself, people would talk if I let them address me only by Sarah. I do, after all, live a lot of my life in public scrutiny. Only my maids in waiting call me Sarah, and only in the privacy of my chambers. Otherwise, the palace staff call me Madam."

"I see," Emmeline responded. "I was asking because it's been a question I've been ruminating for a while now. I attempted to persuade my wait staff to address me just as Emmeline when I was a child, but my governess was quick to rid me of that notion claiming it was improper. Sarah, I—I would be greatly obliged if you would enlighten me as to how improper you think such an act would truly be. I do not see any error in it, but..."

Sarah smiled at the wide-eyed young lady. "Well, Emmeline... I suppose we must begin by discussing what you would consider to be 'improper' to begin with." She gestured towards the plate of pastries on the table between them. "Before that, however, would you fancy a crumpet?"

A/N Hola everyone!

1: Technicalities - Some of you may have noticed the torrent of updates to old chapters. The edits mostly involve an error on my part regarding forms of address - I've altered the story to be more historically accurate, although I still cannot guarantee complete accuracy or credibility. Emmett, for example, should not be addressed as Lord Lockhart; his actual title ought to be Lord Portsmouth, after the territory he is earl to (Portsmouth). Similarly, William should be called Duke Mayfair / Lord Mayfair. Emmeline on the other hand does not have any title of her own but should not go by Lady Lockhart, but by Lady Emmeline.

2: Title - In view of the discovery of the abovementioned inaccuracy, a change to the title is now necessary. So that'll be happening together with this update, and as a kind of remembrance, the old cover is in the Media section if you (or I) ever want to look at it, haha. XD

3: Comment - Tell me which hemisphere you hail from! :) I live under the equator... If only it lent me some southern charm.

That's all for this update. Thanks for reading, voting and commenting, and the second half of this chapter will be up next Friday!

x Leanne

Chapter Eight - Part Two

AMAZING news: We're at #172 in Historical Fiction as of 11 October, 2016! Things like this make me believe that magic is real! Thank you so so so much!

(Unfortunately, we have since dropped back to the 300s. That's okay, though!)

NEITHER PARTY KNEW HOW LONG THE TWO TALKED, ONE A QUEEN AND the other the daughter of a duke, discussing the definition of propriety and the possibility of an error in societal standards. Emmeline brought the animation and energy of a youth into the conversation, while Sarah introduced a kind of otherworldly wisdom that only came with experience and time.

The evening meal was steadily approaching them and yet they continued with their discussion. At some point Penelope had been invited to join her mistress on the opal sofa, listening politely, learning as much as she could from the debate between the two women she admired the most in the world.

Sarah was fond of Emmeline, more so than she had ever been of any prospective match for her son. It was true that she was not a ravishing beauty, but she was not ugly, only plain. Besides, the brilliance of her mind and the purity of her heart were more than sufficient to compensate for what she lacked in physical attractiveness. She was convinced that her son Alexander could be persuaded to love this girl, and that he would make an excellent king with such an outstanding queen ruling with him by his side.

When it became far too late for Emmeline to attempt to return home safely, Sarah offered her a room for the night and invited her to dine as well as sup with them. It would be a good chance for Alexander – as well as her husband King Alexander – to get to know her in a more intimate setting. Naturally, Emmeline could not turn the Queen down, and accepted shyly with a grateful smile.

Greta returned to the drawing room and led Emmeline and Penny to a guest room, where Penny assisted her mistress in bathing and reapplying her powders. Although they had not brought any of Emmeline's toilette, the palace had a steady supply of anything a woman could ever need, and the pair spent much time gushing over the exquisite soaps and creams at their disposal. When Emmeline was ready to be dressed for dinner, Penny sent for a seamstress, who arrived armed with three dresses for the lady to choose from. Emmeline selected the plainest garment, a simple lilac gown, and Penny helped her into it before the seamstress altered it on the spot so that it fit her like the white gloves the seamstress also provided her with.

"You look beautiful, my lady," Penny observed with a slight smile. Beside her, the seamstress nodded her agreement most vigorously.

Emmeline just laughed in response. "Did we not concur at tea that you would call me Emmeline now? If you remember, I made a pact with Queen Sarah. She will let her maids in waiting call her by her name in public if I let you call me by mine, and I am keen to see the results of this little experiment."

The seamstress's eyes widened at this news, but she said nothing.

"Oh, my lady, I could not do so," Penny admitted. "I truly do look up to you as my mistress... It would do you no justice to simply address you by your name."

"Come now, Penelope, cease this ridiculousness," she answered with a light laugh, "do I not call you by your given name as well?"

Penny tried to argue, but she was, after all, in a subordinate position and grudgingly gave in. When Emmeline turned to thank the seamstress, she was already gone – she had long since fled the room, fancying herself unable to hear any more of the Queen's lack of judgement and Lady Emmeline's lack of propriety. Penny frowned at the seamstress's rudeness at leaving without a single word, but Emmeline just chuckled and told her to call for Greta. They had to be taken to the dining hall immediately or they would be late for dinner, and the very last thing Emmeline wished to do was to leave a poor impression on the royal family.

When they arrived in the dining hall – which had no doors leading into or out of it, only a large arches that led to hallways and marked where the enormous room's boundaries began and ended – the entire family was present, seated at the front of a long table that could fit the entire peerage.

"Your Majesties, Your Royal Highness, Lady Emmeline Lockhart of Portsmouth has arrived," Greta announced, her voice ricocheting off the walls of the vast hall. All three heads at the table turned to look, and Emmeline rushed into a curtsy.

"Oh, do rise, my dear," Sarah said warmly. "Come and be seated now – I should very much like to introduce you to my husband and son."

Emmeline obeyed, but sank into another curtsy when she arrived at the table as she greeted the trio. "Good evening, Your Majesty. Your Highnes s... Sarah."

"You permitted her to call you Sarah?" the King hissed indiscreetly upon hearing the young lady speak, and she flushed a deep shade of red, keeping her head down and not daring to rise from her curtsy. She felt her heart begin to wither at the thought of having offended the King – she would be lucky to return home with her head intact now.

"Yes," his wife responded sharply. "You know this, Andrew, all my old friends call me Sarah."

"This lass does not look like an old friend of yours – she looks barely twenty!"

"You great oaf, did I not tell you that Emmeline is Bethany's niece? How on earth could I demand that Bethany's most treasured niece call me Your Majesty? Beth never put on any airs with me—"

"Emmeline Lockhart is your name?" Another male voice spoke, and Emmeline, with her head bowed, could only assume it was the crown prince Alexander.

The queen spoke again, sounding quite exasperated. "Yes, child, did I not inform you also—"

"Well, Lady Emmeline, please rise," Alexander said with a slight edge to his voice as he interrupted his mother for the second time that evening, "and pardon my father's lack of manners as well as my mother's lack of attentiveness."

Emmeline almost sighed in relief as she rose. Her legs were starting to ache quite agonisingly, and upon finally being granted liberty to stand, they screamed sweet relief. However she merely smiled demurely at the prince, and in the measured, dainty tone of a well-bred lady, said, "Thank you, Your Highness, but I must correct you. Your mother has been most kind to me, and it would be unfair for me to imply anything otherwise."

"You are challenging me, then?" the prince demanded, his eyebrows lifting a fraction of an inch and his crystalline blue eyes remaining dispassionate.

Emmeline did not know how much she had offended him – his impassive gaze was rather unreadable – but she knew she must have at least irritated him, and she felt her heart stop beating in her chest for a split second. She cursed herself inwardly for having a knack for offending royalty, but just as she was about to open her mouth to apologise profusely, Alexander spoke again.

"Well, my lady, you are quite an interesting character. Please, have a seat – dinner will be served shortly."

"Thank you, Your Highness," Emmeline responded quietly. As she slid into the chair opposite the prince and next to Sarah, she turned to sneak a glance at the Queen, hoping to see how she felt about this entire situation or – even better – to send out some kind of plea for help. Yet she found her merely observing the entire exchange with a slight smile and a look of glee in her eyes.

For a while nobody said anything; then King Andrew broke the silence in his grave voice: "Welcome to the palace, Lady Emmeline; I trust your stay has been pleasant thus far?"

"Oh, yes, Your Majesty," Emmeline said hurriedly. "Your staff has been most kind to me. I must mention Greta in particular; she has been my guide around your lovely home, and she is wonderfully pleasant."

"Greta takes to you?" Alexander remarked. "Hmm. Interesting."

"Interesting?" Emmeline found herself brave enough to clarify, "how so?"

"Ah, you see, Greta has served in the palace since I was born. She has never been...wonderfully pleasant, as you put it, to our guests. However, she seems to have made an exception with you," he answered. "Do you not find this interesting?"

"I do, Your Highness," she replied, although a slight frown telling of doubt and confusion remained on her face. "Interesting, indeed." Then, after a brief pause, "What, then, do you think of Greta?"

"I think very highly of her, for she is like the mother I never had," was his icy reply. Sarah shifted uncomfortably next to him. Sensing this, Emmeline opened her mouth to change the subject, but he was already elaborating on his statement. "She shows me affection without constantly reminding me that I have to be good enough to someday be king. She loves me, I think, for who I am...not who I have to be."

"Your Highness—"

"Lady Emmeline," Alexander interrupted, a fire coming alight in his eyes and taking Emmeline by surprise. "I know you are here because my mother wishes to make me wed you. I think you are a most fine lady, with plenty of sense and with plenty of your own good opinions. But however much I respect you, my lady, I'm afraid we will never be more than friends."

With that, he stood, bowed slightly, and left the dining hall.

A/N Hi everyone! I hoped you liked the chapter!

Here's the situation: I'm currently not in my city of residence, and this is a pre-written note. Not to worry - I'm spending my free time fruitfully, i.e. writing the sequel to Artemis (exciting stuff, eek!), which will be out (pretty much immediately) after all chapters have been uploaded. Look for news in the Afterword, which will be out after the last chapter (Chapter 20).

I digress! As I meant to say - you're reading this memo on the date it's meant to be published thanks to my very lovely friend who's taking the trouble to upload this, so you have her to thank for that! :) That aside, I do have one announcement to make:

Splitting Chapters - I'll be splitting some chapters up if (i) they are 2500-3000 words long and (ii) they can be split up evenly and cleanly. Since I post every week, I'm not sure if it's a good idea to be posting really long chapters each time anyway, so we'll see how this goes. This will be a thing for Chapters Eight and Nine, and I might consider doing it more after I get back from my trip (I'll be uploading personally again at around Chapter Fourteen. It's an insanely long time to be away, but it's more of a matter of necessity.). Let me know if you like (or dislike!) the idea, and we'll either continue it or terminate it based on reader response.

As usual vote, comment, and follow! Even if I don't have access to Wattpad in the country I'm visiting, I'll be checking in with my friend on how we're doing every now and then! #172 is fantastic, but I do hope there's even more good news to come! :)

Thanks everyone!x Leanne

Chapter Nine - Part One

K ING ANDREW SIGHED HEAVILY. "I APOLOGISE, LADY EMMELINE. YOU, AS A guest, should definitely not have witnessed thus an unpleasant scene... My son has been especially ill-behaved of late."

"Oh, I assure you it is no matter, Your Majesty," Emmeline dismissed hurriedly, "but shall no one go to comfort His Highness? He appeared...upset."

The King shook his head with a chuckle, but even his laugh was stony. "No. It is useless pursuing that boy when he is upset, Lady Emmeline. He is absolutely inconsolable and, to speak candidly, utterly beyond reason."

"My husband is correct," Sarah quipped. "I must, however, say in Alexander's defence that his character is very much inherited from his father."

"What nonsense," Andrew refuted. "I am perfectly level-headed."

"Impassive, perhaps, but hardly level-headed," she disagreed, "and completely unreasonable when provoked."

Emmeline squirmed in her seat, unsure if this subtle argument was a harmless lover's quibble or a symptom of a broken marriage. Andrew noticed this out of the corner of his eye and responded to his wife with, "Come now Sarah, you make the Lady uncomfortable." Then, in his thundering voice, he commanded, "Bring the first course to the table!"

The meal began to be served, and Emmeline would have staggered at the grandiose of it all if she had not been seated in that throne-like chair. There were salads and soups and lamb and beef and venison, and for dessert she was presented with a plate of beautiful sweets originating, the King informed her with a self-important look upon his countenance, all the way from India. Sarah's chatter filled the entire meal, with King Andrew remaining terrifyingly silent and Emmeline only responding politely when absolutely necessary. She did not wish to come across as out of line before the King any further than she already had, and was determined to remain proper as can be for the rest of the evening. Even after all the plates had been cleared, however, Sarah seemed eager to talk. Eventually the King retired to his chambers and left Emmeline alone with her, but the Queen did not seem to be affected by this in the slightest – in fact, she began to speak with greater gusto, and Emmeline thought their conversation might never end.

When she was finally escorted back to her room with Penny by her side, the hour could be described as ungodly and Emmeline's eyelids were jousting with one another as she wrestled her fatigue, pushing back yawn after unladylike yawn. Yet, after Penny helped her out of her gown, into her night shift, and eventually into bed, she found herself sleepless.

A lone beam of pale moonlight snuck into the room through a crack in the thick curtains, and Emmeline tossed and turned by herself. Penny had been put up in a small adjacent room meant for maids in waiting right through the service door. Normally her insomnia brought her loneliness; but on this silent night she found herself without the capacity to think of her aloneness as she brooded instead over her marital affairs.

Captain Jamison was the man she would like to be with. Yet her Aunt Beth seemed not to care very much for this information as long as she was not in love with the officer; and when Bethany Rutherford set her mind to doing something, she always saw it through. Emmeline felt her stomach twist at the thought of her aunt's unwavering resilience.

Emmeline could not possibly speak to either monarch about her position; for neither of them were responsible for securing her happiness. She could only approach Bethany, who seemed to be out of the question, or her brother. She felt a tinge of comfort in her heart at the memory of all the things her brother had done for her: arguing with Miss Paltrow to get her out of trouble; dancing with her numerous times at the balls they attended so that she did not have to feel so lonely; arranging for violoncello lessons for himself such that he might, in turn, teach her. The thought of the stately Emmett Lockhart's brotherly protection warmed her from her head to her toes, and it was with this thought in her mind that her heartbeat finally slowed and she found sweet slumber.

***

THE COCKEREL AT LOCKHART MANOR ALWAYS CROWED LATE.

The multiple cockerels at the palace, it turned out, signalled the start of the day quite ahead of time, and Emmeline was awoken by their screeches before the sun had even emerged from the horizon, pushing away warm linens and stretching out from the faraway line that divided earth and sky.

She stretched; then although awake she allowed herself a moment to simply rest in the morning serenity, nestled in sheets and only breathing. Her mind was still this morning, she she was happy to savour this peace. She would rise properly for the day when Penny came to wake her – whenever that might be.

Emmeline was just about to grow restless when the service door opened with a timid creak. Then there was silence again, and Emmeline did not fight the amusement off her lips. "Come in, Penny, I am quite awake. And good morning to you."

"Good morning, my lady," Penelope greeted, sounding slightly meek. She hoped her mistress had not waited long...

"The cockerels here crow quite a bit earlier than ours," she remarked, sitting up. She swung her legs over the side of the bed and into a pair of slippers. As she stood, she made direct eye contact with the maid and asked, "They started to call before sunrise. Did you notice?"

Penny nodded vigorously. "Yes, of course, my lady." An awkward pause. Then, "I do wonder why our cockerels crow so much later in the morn."

"All a matter of habit, I imagine," Emmeline answered with a wink and a laugh. The maid in waiting smiled sheepishly but said nothing else; and they began the arduous task of bathing, dressing, and powdering. After she had been made presentable, Emmeline was led to the throne room to bid the King and Queen goodbye before leaving the castle and returning home. She could hardly wait to return to Portsmouth. For all the splendour and beauty of the castle, the charming small town was still her one and only home, and she was excited to return. This time she would have her brother with her, and perhaps Captain Jamison would call on them both. The thought of the young officer made her stomach flutter, and she was beaming when she entered the throne room.

Sarah's spirits matched hers, and queen seemed happy to see her again. King Andrew, on the other hand, only appeared happy to see her leave.

"I certainly hope you enjoyed yourself, my dear," Sarah said, and for a moment Emmeline thought she saw tears in her eyes, "I had a most delightful time. You are such wonderful company."

Emmeline smiled and bobbed a curtsy. "Thank you for your hospitality, Queen Sarah." Then, turning to stern monarch, she swept into a deeper curtsy and said, "Sincerely, Your Majesty, thank you, too, for a most splendid dinner."

Andrew responded with only a nod. Just as Emmeline was struggling to come up with some kind of response to his silence, Sarah rushed to fill the silence. "It was so lovely having you. I intend to hold a ball next week, and I insist you be present."

"Oh, thank you, but—"

"I will send the invitation to your father's residence," she said, eyes gleaming. "I trust that you will not return to Portsmouth just yet? I hear you do not visit the city often, and there are so many sights to see..."

Emmeline hesitated. She should not encourage the Queen. It was clear to her that the monarch aimed to make a match of Prince Alexander and herself. She turned to the King, almost as if she were searching for inspiration, but he too was watching her expectantly. She returned her gaze to Sarah's beseeching eyes and sighed inaudibly before nodding.

"I will remain in London as you wish, Your Majesty."

The queen did not notice the resignation in her voice, and instead chose to berate her lightly over her formal address. If the King was displeasured by this, he did not show any sign of it. Perhaps he too had resigned himself to his wife's friendliness, and had chosen to bicker with her no more. Instead he looked upon her with loving eyes, and for all their squabbles Emmeline had witnessed, she had not seen such deep affection in a man's eyes before.

Sarah however did not seem to notice. Her crystalline blue eyes remained trained, alight, on her prospective daughter-in-law. Yet, the young lady Emmeline could only sweep into a deep curtsy and bow her head, for she could not, regardless of how she tried, muster a smile in return.

Hey! Thanks for reading!

Leave a comment: As of 18/10/16, I see that I have readers in the United States, Canada, the United Kingdom, Sweden, Ghana, Nigeria, South Africa, Pakistan, India, the Philippines, Brunei, and Australia. It's crazy to have such an international audience - but not only does it stun me, it also makes me very curious! For this chapter, flaunt your national pride and tell me where you're from!

As usual, do vote, comment, and follow!

x Leanne

Chapter Nine - Part Two

- -

Bad news: we've taken quite the tumble down to #972. Here's an early chapter in a bid to salvage the situation before we're off the Hot List altogether – please help to get us back up by voting, commenting, and sharing this story with friends! :)

WHEN EMMELINE ARRIVED AT WELLINGTON HOUSE THERE WAS NO ONE there to greet her. The expansive estate was as silent as the death that still roamed its halls poisoned its air, as suffocating as the decay that had rushed in to fill the void Anne Lockhart had left behind once she left the human realm. Her aunt Bethany was likely to be out calling on her city-dwelling friends, her father was probably cooped up in his chambers, and there was a high chance that Emmett was among noble acquaintances at some kind of afternoon party somewhere.

Upon their arrival upon the grounds Penny went ahead, with her mistress's permission, to unpack Emmeline's things and send her worn dresses to the maids to be washed. Then she found herself surrounded by no one but her own solitude, and Emmeline felt the immediate urge to leave, but the thought of walking alone through the city streets seemed unwise to her, and Penny was already halfway through her duties. She felt that it might be unfair to order the maid in waiting to promptly quit her activities just to fulfil her own frivolous wants. Hence she did her best to shake the feeling off, instead deciding to pen an letter she thought very much overdue.

Since she had not packed paper and pen with her from Lockhart Manor, thinking that her trip would be a short one, she would have to proceed to the room that used to be her study in search of writing instruments. If she found none there, she would request for some from her father, who she was sure wrote letters too, or ask one of the maids to run and buy her some from the shops not too far away. She managed to locate her old study only with slight difficulty, and when she pushed the door open, she was astonished to find it furnished identically as how she had left it. For a reason Emmeline did not know, her father had kept her study exactly the way it was, even after she had departed for Portsmouth.

She sauntered into the room, still reeling from her surprise. As she ran her fingers over the familiar table that seemed to have shrunk slightly, another wave of shock washed over her jumping heart; not a speck of dust was left behind on her hands. The duke appeared to have maintained the condition of the room – there was no doubt that it had been cleaned since she left, probably on a regular basis. The only question weighing on the young woman's mind was: why?

Perhaps it was not his doing, Emmeline reasoned with herself as she attempted to find some plausible explanation, perhaps it was the maids who kept it in such good condition. She had always shared a special bond with the servants, and it was entirely possible that they cleaned her study as a means of remembrance after she had left them alone with William Lockhart.

This was, at least, a more likely reason for the excellent upkeep of her childhood study.

She seated herself before her old desk and, with her fingers crossed, opened the drawer in which she always kept her paper supplies. Just as she had hoped, her prized collection of writing paper laid within the drawer, waiting for her to return again. The different colours drew a smile to her face, and she felt an odd warmth seep into her heart when the familiar smells of her scented paper wafted out of the drawer. Her father has given them to her on her twelfth birthday. When they had been gifted to her, she had not thought much of them; but as she grew and blossomed and into a very literate young lady, she quite enjoyed using them when writing to her dearest friends and family. Bethany Rutherford, in particular, received many letters from her written on sweet-smelling paper.

When she, at the age of eighteen, left London for Portsmouth together with her brother in a fit of rage, she had decided not to bring them along with her simply because her father had given them to her. But now, gazing upon them half a decade after the fiasco that had driven away from the city to begin with, she felt as if she was seeing an old friend again for the first time.

Retrieving one of her spare quills and a bottle of ink she did not remember leaving behind at Wellington House, she chose a blue sheet of paper and, with a light smile upon her lips, began to craft a letter.

Dear Captain Jamison

It is with quite some disappointment that I inform you that I have found myself unable to leave the city for another week, as I am obliged to attend a ball Her Majesty Queen Sarah intends to throw. You are quite dear to me, despite the short duration of our friendship, and I had quite wished to see you...

***

WHILE EMMELINE SAT ALONE IN HER STUDY, BETHANY RUTHERFORD AND William Lockhart sat face to face in one of Wellington House's drawing rooms, engaged in a most serious discussion.

"This is good for Emmeline," Bethany argued. "She will enjoy a rich life as a princess. And someday she shall be Queen! Queen! Mayfair, tell me you do not wish for your daughter to be ruler of her own land."

"Indeed, I do wish for her to live with material comforts," was his grave response. "But pray tell, Sister, has she said anything to you about how she feels of this arrangement?"

She paused, and her eyes locked with the duke's icy green ones. She was silent for a moment too long before she finally said, "No, Brother, she has not taken issue with me about this. I can only assume she is happy with my choice for her, you know, if she remains silent. Of course, I will do only what is for her own good—"

"So there is not another man, then?" William questioned.

Bethany's brow became creased. "Why, do you know of one?"

William's stony eyes stayed locked upon her challenging ones for a second before he exhaled, long and deep and sad, and leaned back in his chair.

"... No."

Thanks for reading! Vote, comment, follow - it means the world to me! x Leanne

Chapter Ten

Hey guys! Sorry about the late update; I'm overseas and I forgot to remind my friend to update on my behalf. Hopefully no one's mad though because I updated last Wednesday. :) Either way, sorry about the late chapter and here it is! Hopefully the content makes up for the timing!

So – we're off the Hot List completely. I was so worried this would happen, but now that it has I just want to say that Hot List or not it's such an honor to have your readership and your encouragement as well as your lovely kind words (@LadyRowyn !) Thank you all for being AMAZING!

THE HORSE'S STEEL SHOES CLATTERED TO A STOP AGAINST THE COBBLED road. The man exchanged a brief word with the guards, who gave him directions and saluted him. He returned the gesture before proceeding to walk the path they had pointed out with anticipation rattling in the chambers of his heart.

When he stepped into ballroom, quite fashionably late, it was noisy with the cacophony of a hundred different voices speaking simultaneously, and the orchestra exerted themselves terribly just to compete with the chatter. It had been a long time since the man had attended anything like this. As he matured and his tastes became more refined he had grown to prefer quieter activities like reading maps and writing in his ship log, but this, he thought, he did not quite mind. The jolly atmosphere brought quite some unexpected excitement to his breast, and he was glad he had come. Regardless of what his cruel friend had said...

There were at least twenty dozen dancing ladies, he gauged with an eye trained to count heads, but he only sought to locate one.

"Aye, Peter, how wonderful! You made it!" A familiar voice interrupted his search as a hand clapped his shoulder in a friendly "hello". He turned to return the amiable greeting, a broad grin finding its way onto his face without much difficulty.

"Oh, Tom!" he exclaimed in return. "Sincerely—! Thank you for the invitation. This truly is delightful. Even though I have yet to find her...There are no parties aboard the ship, you know, and I see now that much has been missing from my life."

"Well, I'm glad! Is this not such a jolly event?" Thomas Maxwell remarked. "What music, and what dancing! Oh—I would very much like to introduce you to my lovely wife Diane, if you will excuse me briefly..."

"Of course," Peter said with an obliging smile and a half-bow; and Thomas disappeared into the dancing sea of finery. The two had been closely acquainted schoolmates since they were wee, but eleven; and although Peter later became a seafarer and Tom remained a land-dweller, their bond only strengthened with time. They were each other's faithful correspondents, confidants, and advisors, and no expanse of ocean, no force of nature, no official command could change it. The captain was glad to have such a spectacular friend in his otherwise mediocre life, and the gentleman he could call a dear friend thought the same.

***

"MY, WHAT A PARTY," EMMETT LOCKHART OBSERVED AS HE WALKED INTO the ballroom with his sister on his arm. "Is it not, Linnie?"

The ball was already in full swing when the two arrived. Emmeline's stomach was rocking as if she were on a ship in turbulent waters for the first time and she made no answer. The earl cast her a concerned glance, but said nothing.

"Lord Emmett Portsmouth and Lady Emmeline Lockhart!" the crier wailed, quite mournfully, Emmeline thought to herself with a sad sigh of her own. The Queen, who was perched upon a throne at the front of the room beside her husband and looking rather tired, stood immediately and beckoned the young lady forth with newfound zest.

Emmeline turned to her brother in a silent request for permission to leave his side. He nodded, and with a loving smile, said, "Go ahead, Sister. If you should wish to seek me, I will likely be talking to some friends near the sides of the room. I see quite a few acquaintances, and I imagine they shall not be very pleased if I do not go forth to greet them."

She nodded and bobbed him a short curtsy before weaving through the crowd, then ascending the steps that led to the two gilded seats to come to a stop before the King and Queen. She swept into the customary greeting, and the Queen laughed at the girl's formality. "Rise, my dear."

She complied and beamed at the monarchs. "What a splendid party, Your Majesties. One of the best I have seen."

"I will agree with you, Lady Emmeline, that Sarah gives excellent parties," King Andrew answered with amicability that almost frightened her. "This must be one of her best yet, and, you know, she gave it for you."

"Oh!" Emmeline was quite at a loss for words, and all she could think to do was curtsy again before she found something else to respond with. "What an honour... I am hardly worthy, Your Majesties, but thank you."

"My dear, do rise," Sarah said.

Emmeline complied, and she spoke again. "Well, Emmeline, I think I should let you know that I had a word with Greta. Oh dear me, she praised you straight to the high heavens."

A slight crease formed in the young lady's brow. "I don't understand..."

"Greta... Well, she is something of an informant for me." She smiled sheepishly. "I have had her speak with each of the ladies I am considering to be my son's future wife, you understand, so that I am able to truly know these young women. I would just like you to know that her kind words about you speak volumes, my dear."

"I—I'm not sure what to say," Emmeline replied with a nervous laugh. "Thank you?"

"No, no, do not thank me for merits that are yours. Oh, yes – wherever is your Aunt Bethany, my child? I did send her an invitation, and quite hoped she would attend."

"Ah – my Aunt Bethany sends her regards," Emmeline said, and speaking of the subject of her worries made the knot in her stomach tighten. "She has been quite ill, and I have not spoken to her for a week now. All I have heard from her was a message this morning to thank you for your kind invitation."

"Oh, how dreadful! I do hope she recovers speedily, my dear."

As do I, Emmeline wanted to cry out, for how else will I stop myself from marrying your son?

Yet all she did was smile tightly and say courteously, "You have my sincerest gratitudes, Your Majesty. I will convey your well-wishes to my aunt."

"You will call me Sarah, dearest," the kind-eyed queen said. Then, with a mischievous glint in her eye, she added, "If Andrew frightens you, pray pay him no mind. He is far too uptight, you know, for my liking anyway."

The King cleared his throat and straightened in his throne, a frown etched into his face, but said nothing. Emmeline swallowed a bemused giggle, and Sarah outrightly laughed. He remained silent still, but Emmeline caught a glimpse of a hint of a smile at the corners of his mouth, and that only tickled her more. It was clear that, despite their differences in personality, he loved his wife dearly; and if her playfulness was any indication of her sentiment towards him, she felt the same way. All she wished for, the young lady thought to herself, was a marriage so full of love.

"You ought to be dancing, Lady Emmeline," the King said after a short silence, "not standing here talking. You are a young lady at a party. Go. Alexander is dancing, too, and will claim a dance from you the moment he is able to."

His good-natured tone turned even Sarah to face him with shock, and it took Emmeline three beats too long to react. When she finally recovered from her surprise, she laughed somewhat sheepishly and rushed into a curtsy. "Of course, Your Majesty. Thank you."

He accepted her gratitude with no words but a kind nod. After bobbing a final curtsy for good measure, Emmeline proceeded down the steps and into the sea of dancing colours. Emmeline kept her eyes trained on the marble flooring to avoid tripping over a foot – or anything else that may have lain abandoned – and tried to navigate through the crowd. She was halfway across the room when she felt a presence in front of her, and had to lift her eyes. Prince Alexander, she thought it must have been; I wonder if—

"Captain Jamison!" she cried, before hurrying to offer him a curtsy.

"Fancy seeing you here, Lady Emmeline," he greeted with a chuckle, and bowed in return. "I was hoping you could spare me a dance."

"Oh, I'm not sure I could," were the words that accompanied her cheeky grin.

"I insist," he said with a glint in his eye. "May I have your dance card, my lady?"

Emmeline sighed melodramatically. "Since you are so persistent, I suppose I have no choice in the matter." Then she laughed, and handed him her card. "I jest. I would be glad to dance with you, Captain."

Pencil in hand, he filled his name in for three dances in a row. When he returned her the card, her eyebrows were lifted questioningly.

He shrugged, as if completely helpless, and said, "I have missed you, Lady Lockhart."

"As I you," she said, her cheeks turning rosy.

"May I have this dance?" He extended a hand to her with a light in his eyes.

Smilingly, she slipped her gloved hand into his. "You may."

***

THEY DANCED UNTIL THEIR FEET BEGGED FOR REST, THEIR MUSCLES screaming with exhaustion; and yet when they finally left the dance floor arm-in-arm at the end of three dances they were both beaming at one another. Their bodies were tired but their minds did not seem to register their exertion, and their eyes continued to dance with energy as they conversed.

"That was lovely," Emmeline exclaimed, breathless. "Are you certain you do not spend all your time dancing, Captain Jamison? You are quite good at it."

Peter laughed. "You flatter me, Lady Emmeline, but I only seemed talented because my partner was the best in the room to be had."

"I never flatter," she answered pointedly with a teasing smile ghosting across her lips, "only speak the truth. You know, Sir, many say that Emmett is wonderful at dancing, and I have had the privilege of sharing many a dance with him. As a person familiar with his level of skill, I pronounce you equally proficient."

He grinned at her as they came to a stop in a quieter corner of the room. "I am honoured, my lady. Not only for your compliment, but also for your permission to claim so many dances. It was most magnanimous of you to sacrifice your time so."

He bowed deeply, and she curtsied with a giggle. "The pleasure was mine."

"Shall I fetch you a beverage?" he offered. "I think I should quite fancy one right now."

"Yes, pray do so," she replied with an eager nod.

"What would you like? I hear there is quite a variety of choices tonight."

"A ratafia, please. I will await you – and my beverage – here."

With a nod and one last doting smile, he vanished into the crowd. Even after he had left her, however, Emmeline found it impossible to wipe the joy from her countenance. She had never been in such close proximity with the captain before, and for the first time she noticed the exact shade of his eyes: a warm hazel that made her heart feel as if it was being coated in warm caramel. He made her feel like a precious gemstone, almost like the way her brother gave her security and affection, and it was impossible for her not to crave more of his attentions. As she waited, and still smiling, she shifted he weight from foot to aching foot and wondered when he would return to her side with her ratafia.

In her boredom, she eventually turned to examining the detailing on the pillars in the room. Every inch of the palace was intricately built and decorated, and she could not conceal her awe at the planning and effort that must have gone into the construction of this grand home. She thought the gold inlay where the pillar met the ceiling quite—

"Lady Emmeline Lockhart."

A familiar masculine voice broke her reverie. Her name was spoken like a command, and she began to feel a strong sense of dislike for the person who had chosen to say it in such a demeaning fashion. She turned, only to come face to face with the nation's prized crown prince, and it was with much difficulty that she forced the smile to remain upon her face.

"Your Highness." Her voice was saccharine, and she swept into a curtsy so low it was almost sarcastic in nature. "How may I be of service?"

"Rise," he said, sounding bored and even disdainful. "I require a dance from you, Lady Emmeline."

"I'm afraid I am currently waiting for a friend, Your Highness," she replied, but his tone had ignited a fire within her that had her eyes blazing in defiance, completely unapologetic. "I apologise. Perhaps later?"

"Tell me, what is your game, my lady?" the prince sneered.

Emmeline cocked her head. "Excuse me?"

"What exactly is your plan, Emmeline Lockhart? Do you wish to have me exiled – is that your grand aim? First you gain my parents' favour, then you make my father command me to dance with you, to court you, and you refuse so that I look like a rebellious son. Is that your game?"

He had misunderstood her sorely – she saw that now. But this was hardly the time to clear the air with the prince. Considering his temperament, evidence of which she had noticed at dinner with the the royal family the previous week, discussing this issue now would only create a scene before London's most noble folk.

Thus, she took a breath, looked him levelly in the eye, and made a calm a response as she could muster. "Your Highness, pray do not misunderstand. I do not deny you the permission to dance with me," she answered pointedly, arching an eyebrow. "I only ask, most respectfully, that you allow me some time. It will not be polite, proper, nor pleasant for my friend to return, only to find me missing from the place I promised to stay at."

Alexander's brow crumpled in irritation, and his piercing, fiery gaze remained fixed on her determined mien for a good amount of time before he finally spoke again. "Do you wish to displease my father?"

"Of course not, Your Highness, but, from my interactions with him, I do think His Majesty is a fair, just and reasonable man. He will understand my position. I appeal to you to do the same. No blame nor exile will befall you, Your Highness."

Prince Alexander was silent again, but his frustrated breaths are audible. He regarded her with venom in his eyes for a few moments before finally seizing her wrist. "Dance with me. That is not a request, Lady Emmeline, it is an order."

"Unhand me!" she hissed, but there was no response from him as he hauled her to the middle of the dance floor. He raised his head with rage burning in his eyes, and when Emmeline followed his glare she found him looking directly into King Andrew's eyes. The King offered him a slow and steady nod, perhaps not noticing how angry the young prince was. Now that he was sure his father had seen him following instructions, he looked back down at Emmeline. She averted her eyes immediately.

She had never seen such poison in any person's eyes, and it almost frightened her to be trapped in his arms.

How could she marry this man?

A/N Hi everyone! I'm trying media out in this chapter! I used to be a HUGE Taylor Swift fan and I absolutely love Starlight! I thought of it when I was editing this chapter so check the song out if you don't already know it!

Media: Yay or nay? Let me know in comments below!

Note - This is a pre-written Author's Note in preparation for my upcoming travel. I may or may not be the one uploading, so I consequently may or may not respond within a short period of time. Still, I will read through all your lovely comments when I get back, so do leave word so that I know you were here! :)

x Leanne

Chapter Eleven

Hi everyone! Sorry this is late – as you may remember, I'm not in my city of residence and I couldn't connect to WiFi. Here's this week's update, but before that, a quick message.

On 31 October, the same day as the last update (also, in fact, Halloween), we skyrocketed back up to #271 after being completely wiped off the Hot List. I must say however that the numbers don't mean half as much to me anymore. I'd just like to say an earnest thank you to every single reader, everyone who votes, everyone who comments. Thank you. Hot List or not, you make my day every time. :)

"AUNT, I WAS HOPING TO HAVE A WORD WITH YOU." THE TONE OF Emmeline's voice was far firmer than Bethany Rutherford has ever heard it, and the marchioness was forced to sit up in bed and finally engage in this dreaded conversation. Still, as she did so, she coughed violently for good measure.

"Yes, my dear?" she wheezed.

Emmeline sighed. "I have been putting this discussion off for some days, Aunt, especially since you have been...so unwell. Yet I am to leave for

Portsmouth in two days and you shall return to Rutherford House... I must not delay this any further."

Bethany nodded, prompting the girl to elaborate.

"I would like to discuss my marriage with you, Aunt Bethany," she explained. "I do not think I should like to marry Prince Alexander."

The older woman's eyebrows shot to her hairline. "Why ever not?"

"I am... Well, you could say that I am not very fond of him," Emmeline said cautiously. "He has been rather unpleasant. You told me earlier I might grow to like him, but truly, Aunt, I have not at all."

"Oh, darling – if you marry this man, you will one day be queen," Bethany replied with the enthusiasm her niece should have had. "Your life will be perfect!"

Emmeline shook her head. "Aunt, you do not understand. Prince Alexander – he is quite impolite, and jumps so quickly to conclusions. With no evidence to speak of, he has somehow formed the opinion that I wish to have him exiled, and he hates me for it. Oh, Aunt Bethany, you know I would do no harm to him, and yet he detests me so! How could I marry him?"

"My goodness!" she exclaimed. "Exiled, you say?"

"Is that notion not ridiculous? Why would I ever wish to see him exiled?"

Bethany shook her head regretfully. "Oh, darling, His Royal Highness must have, somehow, misunderstood you gravely. Fret not, for I will most definitely take your side on this and I'm sure Their Majesties will see reason... However, I do think this matter can be resolved without calling the marriage off. My darling Emmeline – your mother, bless her soul, was never here to teach you this, but you must always remember that, as a lady, the solution is never to run away from whatever problems you encounter. Rather, with dignity, intelligence, and grace, always face them bravely, and always do your best..."

The young lady watched her aunt prattle on and on, and said no more; for she knew that there was nothing else she could do to persuade her. She would need to find another way out.

***

EMMELINE'S NEXT LETTER TO PETER WAS WRITTEN IN RELATIVE ELATION, for it told of her impending return to Portsmouth. She had failed to see him ever since Prince Alexander had so rudely pulled her onto the dance floor that evening at the ball, but she had received a letter informing her that he was returning to Portsmouth for a brief stay until his next journey in the high seas. Joy fluttered in her breast as she handed it to one of her father's servants to be sent. The sight of her half-packed luggage brought a smile to her lips again. Perhaps physically leaving London would erase whatever plans had been made for her and Alexander. With some luck, she would be able to stay away long enough, and Queen Sarah might forget all about her...

Emmeline knew, all too well, that she was only deceiving herself. Her aunt was still very much convinced that she should marry the crown prince, and Bethany would never let the royal family forget her name as long as she was thus determined. The young lady had no plan to speak of. A discussion with her maid in waiting yielded nothing, for the young lass, who was little more than a child, could do no else than express her distress at the situation and vow eternal loyalty should Emmeline require any assistance at all.

Upon her return to Portsmouth, Emmeline thought, she was speak with her best advisor Adalberto. Even if he were unable to provide good advice on what she should do about her highly-politicised situation, he would at least be able to offer her some good consolation.

Bethany had recovered from her illness the very night Emmeline spoke with her, and at every opportunity chattered on and on about how luxurious her niece's life would be once she was crowned princess. During one specific conversation in the drawing room the day before their departure for Portsmouth, Emmett too seemed rather thrilled by the prospect, and appeared particularly smug each time Bethany praised him for seeking her help in the first place. Although she felt sick to the stomach watching him smile so, Emmeline said nothing. After all, how could she tell him that she did not wish to go through with the match he and her aunt had worked to secure because she was in love with the man he had warned her against falling in love with?

Emmett had always been a supportive brother, glad to assist her in pursuing her endeavours such as the violoncello. However, he had always made one boundary very clear. She remembered asking once at dinner about the friend who always called on them, the friend whom she would occasionally curtsy to in the hallway. He smiled gently at her in that elder-brotherly fashion that always made her feel so safe. He told her that his name was Peter Jamison, that he was a naval officer – and that she should never take an interest in him romantically. "He will not make you happy," Emmett had said, his typically jovial eyes stern. "He is always sailing. Emmeline, I am certain that you do not wish to be a wife who spends her life waiting for her husband."

"No," she had said, then still but a girl of ten and seven, "I want to be happy, brother." Then, he had seemed satisfied, and promised her that he would seek her a lovely marriage; and yet in the present day she found herself thinking that only Captain Jamison could bring her bliss in this lifetime.

Adalberto had told her once that Emmett would support whatever could bring her happiness, and she too believed that he would. Perhaps then, she should simply tell him. Before, she worried that she would upset him by directly disobeying his previous orders; but since he seemed to eager to guarantee her a happy life, she was now quite certain that he would not mind it. She believed, in the deepest corners of her soul, that Emmett would fight for her happiness – he would tell their Aunt Bethany that she did not want to marry Alexander, and perhaps that would resolve it all.

"Emmett." She hardly noticed that she had halted Bethany abruptly in the middle of her sentence. "May I speak with you, in private?"

"Certainly," Emmett replied; then, with an apologetic glance towards Bethany, he said, "Excuse us, Aunt Bethany. Apologies – I will be glad to hear all about your schooldays the moment I finish my conversation with Linnie."

Their aunt seemed adequately appeased, and nodded. The duo left with a curtsy and a bow, retreating to a quiet hallway.

"What is it, sister?" Emmett's voice was patient and caring, which boosted Emmeline's confidence immediately.

"Brother, you understand," she began, "I do not wish to marry Alexander."

"Why on earth would that be the case, my dear?" he exclaimed. "His Royal Highness is the most eligible—"

"He may be crown prince, Emmett, but he is not the man for me."

Emmett stood in silence, simply studying her face for some time before speaking again. "Should I seek you another match, then? I am sure—"

"No," she said, and for a reason she could not explain yet she was grinning now. "No, Emmett."

"I will respect your decision, Linnie, but I think you should reconsider if you mean to say that you wish to remain unmarried for the rest of—"

"No," she said, taking his hands in hers. "Emmett, there is...someone."

"Is that the case, now?" He pulled his hands out of hers, but she hardly noticed him do so as she kept on smiling. "What is his name?"

"Oh—it is Captain Jamison," she said. "Peter."

Emmett's expression grew dark, and he exhaled heavily. "Emmeline, you have always been such a lover of love, a lover of all. I knew you would fall for his manner, you know, and that is why I specifically warned you against him. Have faith in my words, sister, you cannot marry a navy-man. I am aware that Peter is a very charming man, and that many girls tend to take an interest in officers for some strange—"

"No!" she exclaimed. "Oh, Emmett, you misunderstand. Captain Jamison is not only charming, but he is the most wonderful man I have met – second only to you."

"Linnie, tell me – have you seen him of late? Perhaps after you left Portsmouth?" His voice was gentle like it always was, but there was a hardness to his eyes that Emmeline had never seen in her life. It felt like a threat, and it frightened her. There was something strange about the way he was acting. There was something about him she did not know. This did not feel like her beloved older brother at all.

She thought of Peter claiming three dances from her at the ball. She thought of the laughter they had shared. She thought of his wonderful hazel eyes.

Then, she said, "No. Should I have? Is he is London?"

Emmett exhaled, and she could not tell if it was in frustration or relief. "Emmeline—do you remember what I told you? If you marry him... You will be a woman always waiting. I do not wish for you to have a husband who will never be near you, who will never make you happy. Truly... You know this, dear sister. All I want is for you to be happy."

"Captain Jamison makes me happy," she argued.

"Perhaps now he does, while he courts you," was his answer, "but this will not be forever. He will break you like Father ruined our mother, and... Do you understand?"

"Oh, Emmy, I promise he shall not! I am unable to explain this, but I can feel it in the marrow of my bones – he will not hurt me."

"Quit this silliness – you cannot feel bone marrow." He ran an exasperated hand across his face. "And you have met him only twice, sister. Your confidence in him is baseless. You know that he is my dearest friend, and I will defend him to the death...but his physical absence is no flaw to a friend. If you should come to love him – if you should become his wife, he will become your entire world. His frequent trips will make your life excruciating, Linnie. I cannot allow him to hurt you so."

Emmeline was silent for a minute. Then,

"What if I am willing to be hurt?"

"Nonsense, Sister. As long as my heart continues to beat, I will never let anyone hurt you."

"Emmett, this discussion is not about—"

"Enough. If your cause for leaving His Highness is so that you might marry Peter, Emmeline, I apologise for this, but I will not appeal to Aunt Bethany on your behalf. It may not seem like it, but trust me – I am helping you."

Then he simply walked away from her, and for the first time in many, many years, Emmeline had cause to cry.

***

EMMETT DID NOT SPEAK A WORD TO HER FOR DAYS UPON THEIR RETURN TO Portsmouth. He remained firmly locked in his study during the daylight hours, drowning himself in whatever work earls did anyway. Emmeline has never thought it possible for him to busy himself to that extent. All his meals were delivered to him so that he never had to venture out into common spaces to dine. Should he have to pass her by, he kept stubbornly mute. He made no move to speak to her, and it broke her heart, but she could not find the courage to seek him out either. She had, after all, been the one to bring him great disappointment. She knew that he had thought of her as a wonderfully sensible girl and trusted her to make wise decisions; and that, in allowing herself to start to fall for Peter Jamison, she had annulled a great deal of his faith in her.

Emmeline received a letter from Bethany inviting the siblings to luncheon in her estate in Whitehall, but lacked the will to write back. Penelope made multiple attempts to comfort her, but she was inconsolable. Adalberto was very sympathetic to her situation, but even his kind words offered little comfort. After all, the one constant pillar of support in her life had disappeared from beneath her feet, so quickly that she had been caught entirely off-guard. It was as if she were mourning the loss of a brother – for he had, mostly, vanished from her life in the way her father had many a year ago.

Previously, Portsmouth had been a haven for her. It had a place where she was always able to find love, warmth and security amidst the tumultuous storms that life threw her way. Her brother's property was, to her, the loveliest home she had ever beheld. Yet, after days of life in the dark shadow of her brother's displeasure, each day in Lockhart Manor became a chore to get through, and she began to find even the most unremarkable parts of the mansion quite depressing.

She longed for her old life again. Yet there was nothing much she could do to solve the situation – not without forgoing Captain Jamison and all the joy he brought to her. She was not certain that she could simply let all the happiness he had shown her go; at least, she was unable to make that decision with such immediacy.

It was for these reasons that, a few days later, Emmeline found herself agreeing with little hesitation when the her aunt wrote her again with an invitation to London for another of the Queen's soirées yet.

Chapter Twelve

"MY LADY," PENELOPE SAID, SLIGHTLY QUAKING VOICE BETRAYING HER nervousness as the mistress and servant sat in a carriage on their way into the city, "I do not mean to pry, or to be rude, but do you think—do you think there could exist a possibility that Lord Portsmouth has...another reason for refusing to allow you to marry Captain Jamison?"

"Why ever might you think that that would be the case?" The maid-in-waiting's worry was for naught, for Emmeline did not appear offended in the least. As she prompted the Penny for an elaboration, sounding interested at something at last for the first time in far too many days, she straightened slightly in her seat.

"Well, I know nothing for certain, for I have not seen nor heard anything...yet I have been thinking of this—of course I have the utmost trust for His Lordship, but the more I ponder over them the less his assertions seem logical... If you truly were to marry the captain, and he is indeed sent away frequently, what is to stop you from accompanying him on his voyages? Who is to dictate that you shall be a woman always waiting? Surely His Lordship would have considered this – he is highly intelligent, more so than I will ever be; if this solution came to me, he would, doubtlessly, also be able to conceive it. Although it is true that it is uncommon for wives of sailors to accompany their husbands on board, Lord Portsmouth will probably pay existing norms little attention – he is, after all, exceptionally progressive. He does endorse your pursuit of the violoncello."

Emmeline listened to the explanation intently. While it was unlikely that certain members of the ton would allow her to travel with Captain Jamison without any backlash, Penny made a fair point. Emmett always spoke on the matter as if she had no chance at happiness at all with the captain, and he too had presented valid arguments; but he never seemed to even attempt to come up with solutions for potential problems that might surface. As Bethany had said to Emmeline, on the same subject of her marital affairs—the solution is never to run away from whatever problems you encounter. Rather, with dignity, intelligence, and grace, always face them bravely, and always do your best...

Emmett had always been an adventurer, and never the kind of man to simply quit something the moment he spied a difficulty resting upon the horizon. He jumped headlong into all his riskiest endeavours, always eager to tackle a challenge. He believed in learning by trial and error – he had made his fair share of mistakes, but he always emerged from each event an improved person. He was not a man who worried about the potential cost of seeking happiness – he was not a man who worried about anything. All his life, he had taught Emmeline by example to greet all that life threw their way with a squared shoulders, a raised chin and a grin. His argument, on retrospect, did not fit the man she knew him to be at all.

Yet, her absolute adoration of him meant that she never questioned anything he told her. She never paused to wonder if, perhaps, he was not speaking the truth. Everything he spoke to her had immediately been taken for granted to be true as gospel.

Emmeline could not simply assume that he had been lying. However, she found it inevitable that she began to question – if he had not been truthful to her in providing his reasons against her marrying Peter, why would he have done so? What was his personal stake in her marriage? What concern could he have, if he was not truly worried for her being trapped in a broken marriage the way their mother had been?

The carriage started to rattle noisily as it came onto a cobbled road, echoing the cacophony in her mind. Emmeline sighed as she felt the beginnings of a headache appear in her temples. Whatever Emmett's objectives were... She could think about them when she returned to Portsmouth. Her trip to London was an escape for her. She would not waste it brooding over the twenty-three year long relationship she was questioning for the first time, and over the brother she had deliberately left behind.

***

BETHANY WAS RATHER THRILLED TO SEE HER NIECE AGAIN, IF THE FUSS she made over Emmeline when she arrived was any indication. When she greeted her at the gates of Wellington House, where William had, with surprisingly little resistance, acceded to his daughter's request to accommodate her, she began by asking after her health, for the misery that Emmeline had marinated in for days in Portsmouth had drained much of the colour from her face and the light from her eyes. When she received assurance that the she was mostly well, Bethany ordered the chef to prepare an herbal broth that was supposed to return Emmeline her energy. When it was ready, Emmeline downed it with a grateful smile. Her aunt had always served as a motherly figure to her, and despite the marchioness's lack of sensitivity towards the matters of her heart, she knew that she loved her.

The ball was to be held the day after Emmeline's arrival in London. William graced the two women with his presence the afternoon before the dance, if only to greet his daughter and remind her to inform him if she ever required anything. Emmeline did not know how to respond to his affections, which he seemed especially uninhibited in expressing in Emmett's absence, and only offered a mute nod in reply. For a reason unbeknownst to her, however, her aunt became quite flustered and promptly removed her from the room on the pretext of readying her for the event.

Bethany sent Emmeline off to her chambers to bathe and dress, and, in the meantime, returned to her own chambers to crochet. The young lady Emmeline complied rather eagerly. After her bath, Penny helped her lace her corset and put on her new navy gown. After Emmeline was clean, dressed, styled and made up, she spent a small amount of time reading and only allowed herself to be torn from her book when Bethany, who was as fancily-dressed as always, appeared at the door to summon her to the waiting carriage.

The ride to the palace was filled with Bethany's excited chatter about Alexander and the things she had heard about him. "His Royal Highness will be at the ball tonight, you know," she said to her disinterested niece. "You look beautiful, darling. Perhaps he shall change what he thinks of you this evening."

Perhaps the older noblewoman had delivered her opinion meaning to please, but her words only served to shake her niece, striking her like a mallet to the head. I should not have come to attend this dance, Emmeline thought to herself, regretting her decision. In doing so, I shall only encourage Aunt Bethany and Queen Sarah. I was too eager to flee Portsmouth… I should have considered this more carefully. Yet there was naught she could do about the situation now but make the most of it and attempt to enjoy herself.

"Oh, Aunt, I think not," she hummed absently in reply, opting to look out the window instead of at her aunt. "His mind, I imagine, is quite made up. Besides...It hardly matters to me what he thinks of me or who he thinks I am."

"However might that be the case?" Bethany exclaimed, in shock. "Emmeline, darling, he is to be your husband! It must be importance to you how he views you. Only his good opinion will make your life a happy one."

I will never be happy married to him, she wanted to say. For the sake of politeness, however, she kept silent, instead wordlessly staring at the passing twilight scenery and thinking of how with each second that ticked by her life of freedom and happiness was one second closer to ending.

Yet, there was nothing in the world she could do to stop it.

***

THOMAS MAXWELL FIRST MET HER MAJESTY QUEEN SARAH ON THE DAY HE was born.

As one might expect, he did not remember that occasion; but he had been told of it so many times that he had the sequence of events inscribed in his rock-solid memory; and every time he told it to another curious friend, it still brought traces of a boyish, cocky grin to his face.

She was a solid thirty years of age then; originally only the daughter of a merchant who lived in a small village but princess by way of marriage to the eldest prince. She had returned to her hometown as part of a kingdom-wide tour. She exchanged embraces with old friends and curtsied to the old villagers who had been middle-aged during her childhood.

When she came to stand before the old woman her father had hired to help raise her, she was greeted by a torrent of affection. Then, the old woman told her that a babe had just been born and asked if she would like to see him. Sarah's love of children prompted her to agree with enthusiasm. She entered a decrepit house filled with naught but the cries of an infant and saw a mother dressed in clothes so tattered they may have been rags, desperately trying to quiet it.

The child seemed to know her presence immediately, and was silent the moment the princess stepped into its vicinity. When it saw her face, it smiled.

She found herself quite fond of the wee babe. Without children of her own and with the permission of its mother, she named it her godson, and from then on routinely returned to visit it. As its family had next to nothing to give it, she aided them in raising it by funding everything that it needed. With her help the infant grew into a rosy-cheeked boy who ran and jumped and went to school and bragged to everyone he knew that his godmother was the Queen.

Decades later, Sarah's playful godson grew and climbed the ranks to become a respected member of the gentry named Mr Thomas Maxwell, hardworking, honest and humble. He married a respectable woman, Miss Diane Grey, who bore him two children, a son and a daughter. He named his daughter Sarah and vowed loyalty to the queen for as long as he lived.

When Tom was told of the upcoming palace soirée, he was quite happy, once again, to extend an invitation to his friend. Peter, it seemed, was looking to take a wife; and it was Tom's strong opinion that the young captain had needed a lady in his life for a long time. He had had excellent luck with Diane, who brought him great happiness, and he wished no less than the same for his friend. Thus, he was glad to facilitate his seeking of a suitable bride.

Peter, of course, was exceedingly happy to attend each time Tom's invitations were offered. Though he did not know the reason for it, Emmeline appeared to be on excellent terms with the Queen. Perhaps it was due to the fact that her father was a duke—but, to Peter, the the reasons for the Queen taking to Emmeline did not matter in the slightest. All he cared about was that when Queen Sarah organised dances, the woman he loved was likely to be present; and for that reason alone he was willing to tirelessly attend every party Her Majesty gave, straining his ears to listen out for the crier's voice lest he called Emmeline's name. He was, rather clearly, in love with her.

Thus he was overjoyed, to say the least, when he heard her name again at this soirée. The Queen broke out into a smile, his own lips stretching into a grin when he saw Emmeline step into the ballroom clad in an exquisite shade of navy blue. Navy – He knew it was unlikely, but it was almost as if she had thought of him when she dressed for this party. He wondered if he crossed her mind as often as she crossed his, and continued to grin like a fool as he watched her walk with what, to him, was unparalleled poise across the room and towards a smiling pair of monarchs. Queen Sarah was outrightly beaming at the young lady; and even the typically steely-faced King appeared somewhat pleased to see her, the corners of his lips tilting upwards with such subtlety that the common beholder would not notice it unless he strained his eyes to see.

Emmeline exchanged a brief word with the royal husband and wife. For a while, all three faces turned serious; then the Queen smiled again, and Emmeline curtsied before leaving them. It was then that Peter made his advance and approached her, as he had previously done. He cleared his throat as he came to a stop before her, and the surprise and delight on her face made his heart skip a beat.

"Peter! How lovely it is to see you again!" she exclaimed, her face erupting into a grin. What luck, she thought, that she might encounter him again! "But I must ask—whatever brings you here?"

"Well, someone paid me a compliment about my dancing technique," he said with a teasing glint in his eye, "and I thought I would develop it with practice. Would you be so gracious as to assist me?"

Emmeline laughed, her emerald eyes shining in the light of the chandelier. "Well, Sir, I typically consider myself rather above coaching amateurs, but I suppose I might be willing to help you only because you asked so nicely."

He laughed, but bowed; she curtsied in return, and then they commenced a lively waltz, each sweeping the other off their feet. She forgot about Prince Alexander and Emmett Lockhart vanished from his mind.

As they danced, Emmeline smiled wider than she ever had, and though it was hardly possible, Peter's grin outstretched hers. For the few fleeting moments they shared in one another's arms, all seemed right in the world. Dances were the only place he might meet her without alerting her brother of it; and he would attend every single one he could if it meant only seeing her one more time.

Chapter Thirteen

Happy Saturday (or Friday, for some)! Enjoy the chapter and let me know what you think! x Leanne

WHEN EMMELINE ARRIVED IN HER FATHER'S ESTATE AFTER THE DANCE, she was utterly exhausted. She had danced four times in total with the captain and once with the prince, who, once again, had been quite impolite. Neither, it seemed, wished to dance with the other. She had done her very best to be civil with him regardless of his own manners, and had not said anything particularly out of line, but she could feel her patience with the royal brat wearing thin.

Yet, her encounters with the captain, twice before and twice after she had shared an unpleasant waltz with the prince, erased much of her dissatisfaction and left her in relatively high spirits when she left the ball. When she came through the front door of Wellington House, the entire property was still under the shadow of night, but one of the butlers had been awake awaiting her and came forth to greet her and her maid-in-waiting.

"Good evening, my lady," he said, bowing. "His Grace hopes that you enjoyed the soirée, and wishes to inform you of some exciting news. Lady Adelaide Farthingale, a potential match for Lord Portsmouth, and her father Lord Arthur Coppershire will be visiting Wellington House for supper this week. His Grace has sent for Lord Portsmouth to arrive in London within the next two days, and hopes that this shall please you."

Emmeline tensed for a split second, but composed herself quickly. Skilfully affixing a pleasant smile upon her face, she thanked him courteously and proceeded to walk towards her chambers with added haste. If the young maid noticed her mistress's anxiety upon receiving this piece of information, she said nothing of it, only walking brisk and quiet alongside her. Penelope knew that Emmeline was busy with her own thoughts, and that it would be prudent to speak to her only after she had finished processing the chaos swirling within her own mind.

Meanwhile, the young lady was, once again, ruminating over her own wisdom and foresight. Perhaps London had not been the best place to come away to. She had found little respite here, and only two days after her arrival, her brother, the very person she sought to avoid, would be on his way to live once again under the same roof as her. She wondered if he would still hate her, and if being near him would still make her feel terrible. Perhaps she should simply leave Wellington House and return again to Portsmouth the day he was due to arrive...then she might not have to even see his face at all. Yet she was aware that her father and aunt would likely expect her to attend the meal with the Marquis of Coppershire and his daughter, and she saw no escape in sight.

As Penelope helped her undress and ready for bed, a barely-audible sigh escaped her lips. Perhaps it was simply impossible to flee him. Perhaps this was an arrangement by God's hand. Perhaps she was, whatever her will, meant to face her brother sooner or later.

Sleep that night came with much difficulty, but sometime during the wee hours she finally fell into a fitful slumber, dreaming of Emmett and his two eyes, once holding only love and warmth, burning nightmarishly with an emerald flame of rage and disapproval.

***

NO ONE ELSE MUST HAVE KNOWN OF THE TWINS' CONFLICT, FOR WHEN Emmett Lockhart arrived at Wellington House, Bethany came bustling into his sister's chambers to deliver the "good news". Emmeline, who had been hiding from her brother under her sheets, pretended to be asleep when the older woman came into the room. Penelope, who had received detailed instructions beforehand, informed the older woman that her mistress had been feeling slightly nauseous since rising that morning, and had said that she wished to rest as much as possible so that she was in top form for dinner with Emmett's potential match.

"I see," were the only curt words offered to the maid; then Bethany walked to stand beside her niece and ran a gentle hand over her locks. With a regretful sigh, she left the room, proceeding to fawn over her charming nephew, who was sitting alone in the drawing room. The duke had claimed to have business on the town, and left the estate shortly before his son was due to arrive.

When the sound of her footsteps finally turned into silence, Emmeline sat up with her own sigh, but one of relief. Common courtesy dictated that she would see her brother at the evening meal the next day, but till that time came, she was determined to remain firmly shut in her chambers and avoid him for as long as she possibly could. Hence, fishing one of her books out from under her blanket, she propped up her pillows, leaned back, and began to read.

"My lady," Penny piped up after some silence, "forgive me for being as bold as to say so, but it is my humble opinion that you cannot avoid His

Lordship forever... He is, after all, your brother, and your closest family member..."

Emmeline closed her book and turned to her with a slight smile, her green eyes peaceful with patience and resignation. "You are a lovely lass, Penny, and truly, I thank you for your concern...but I cannot bear to see him so angry with me."

"But, my lady, would an apology not suffice in quelling his ire?"

She shook her head, the slight sway of her long hair telling of sadness she had never experienced before. "How I wish it would be enough... But I know Emmett well, Penny, and he does not seek from me an apology. He wishes me to make a choice. He wishes me to choose between my brother and the man I wish to marry... And I cannot make that decision; at least not today."

"You know, my lady, I quite wonder why he is so insistent," Penny remarked, frowning slightly as she lapsed into deep thought. "He is, after all, usually quite supportive of your wishes."

"Well, you did mention this on the carriage ride into town, but I'm afraid I have thought of no answers yet." Once she had made her answer, the young lady pulled her lips into a tight smile, picking her book up again and signalling the end of the conversation. She had come to London to escape the bad moods her brother brought, and although he had too arrived in town, she would try her very best not to dwell on the issue and sink into another bout of depressiveness. Needless to say, she did not enjoy it, and it would do her no good.

Though she made no other attempt at a reply with the with exception of a dejected hum, the well-oiled cogs and gears in Penelope Smith's young mind were beginning to click and whir.

***

EMMELINE WAS DRESSED IN A LOVELY NEW PURPLE GOWN AND STYLED impeccably for the formal introduction to her potential in-laws when the father and daughter from Coppershire pulled into the Wellington driveway, their family insignia carved into the expensive carriage. Emmeline thought the entire production was slightly gaudy, but kept silent as she stood by her father to greet them at the door. Her comments could certainly wait until after the guests had left their home. Her brother was standing opposite them alongside the twins' enthusiastic aunt. He was stony-faced and dissatisfied, and although it upset her greatly to see him so miserable and so similar to how their father always behaved, it was hardly the occasion to say anything about it.

After pleasantries had been exchanged, one particular individual only slightly more begrudging in offering his welcome than the others, the group of six proceeded to the dining room. Emmett was placed opposite his prospective wife, and Emmeline beside her. On Adelaide's other side was Lord Coppershire, whose eyes reminded Emmeline of a rodent, and despite her better judgement, she found herself assuming he was a conniving man. Bethany, though seated further away from the marquis, had trained penetrating eyes scrutinisingly upon him, deciding for herself if Emmett should indeed gain such a father-in-law.

No one spoke until Adelaide finally piped up, her voice shrill and canary-like, her light eyes beaming at William. "What a lovely residence you have, Your Grace! In such a wonderful location, too!"

"Thank you, Lady Adelaide," he answered gravely. "But my humble abode is hardly worthy of your high praise. I hear that your father, on the contrary, has a beautiful home."

"Oh yes, my lord, that Papa does indeed!" she exclaimed. "There is a lake within the property, which is lovely to look at during twilight, and a marvellous patch of wood where Papa hunts his game! I do think you would enjoy a hunt there, Emmett! Oh, how rude of me, Lord Portsmouth—may I call you Emmett?"

Emmett suffered an embarrassing loss in a battle with scowl upon his face, while his sister fought her laugh with more luck. Bethany Rutherford, who seemed to lose interest in her food, had a disdainful frown fixed upon her face – Adelaide Farthingale's loud, screeching bragging had, undoubtedly, impressed upon her a very poor image of the girl. When she failed to address Emmett in the proper fashion, Bethany's frown only deepened, and her brow furrowed in what could have been perceived as disgust. Only William was successful in maintaining his absolute composure, and with an expression more unreadable than ever, he said to the lively Coppershire girl, "You may call Emmett whatever you wish, my lady."

Bethany's eyes widened in horror as she launched into a coughing fit. She had always known that her brother-in-law was somewhat of a recluse, slightly out of touch with his interpersonal skills, but she had never seen him as an improper oaf! Emmeline, on the other hand, saw humour in the situation and longed to burst out laughing at what she thought was pure insensitivity on father's part, but for the sake of propriety suppressed the urge to giggle. Emmett looked absolutely livid as he glared daggers at his father, who was still an image – the very epitome, in fact – of seriousness and gravity as Adelaide nearly squealed in a bout of excitement.

Inwardly, however, William enjoyed a bout of utter amusement. Emmett would not marry this girl, he knew for certain now; she would frustrate him to his death, and do him no good at all. However, it definitely still was good fun to annoy him so, and so the senior duke had every intention to continue carrying out deliberate acts of sabotage throughout the meal.

This was the most fatherly he had ever felt, and he had his mind set to making the most of the evening.

The food was served, and, as Emmeline predicted, Adelaide dominated the conversation, her golden ringlets bouncing every time she opened her mouth to talk, each time more enthusiastic than the last. Her mousy-haired father contributed the additional comment, which usually involved some kind of praise for his daughter, and while Bethany seemed to aim to strike down everything she said. Emmeline was content to speak only when spoken to, and Emmett seemed content to not speak at all.

All six hosts were quite relieved when the meal drew to a close (even William, who was quite tired of Adelaide Farthingale's high-pitched voice). Once they had seen their guests out of Wellington House, they each declared that they would be returning to their chambers to rest.

Emmett spent his time pacing and restless, enraged with his father; Emmeline laughed about the experience with her maid-in-waiting; William tried, with little success, to think of an alternative match for his son; and Bethany wrote a letter to her royal friend with many comments about the horrible meal. She informed Sarah, determination oozing from every word she penned, of what horrors would befall her nephew if he truly did marry this woman, and of the magnitude of her intention to find him, as she called it, a "proper wife".

She ended her letter with a request for assistance if it could be given, and when the Queen's reply arrived in Wellington House not long after, help was offered.

***

AS EMMELINE GIGGLED WITH PENELOPE OVER ADELAIDE FARTHINGALE'S overtly-lively manner, Peter lay tossing and turning and quite sleepless in an upscale inn in Westminster, thinking, once again, of the same maiden who had haunted his mind for many nights now.

He remembered every detail from the dance – she had been ravishing in her navy gown, and lovely in his arms. He thought of how she had laughed unabashedly and blushed prettily and spoken with that outstanding wit of hers that he admired so much. How he had wished to keep her close to him forever. Yet he released her reluctantly when she excused herself after two dances. Pardon me, Peter, but I have something to attend to. Those had been her exact words. She had curtsied her temporary farewell, and he had bowed in return, still with a smile although he felt chillier than before without her in his arms. She left him with a mischievous glint in her eye, and a thousand butterflies erupted in his gut at the sight of it. If she was an enchantress, he was bewitched, and he could not make himself regret it even if he wished to.

The next Peter saw her, however, she was on the dance floor again; this time not with him but with the country's crown prince. All Peter could think of was – why? Did she not have the same sentiments towards him as he harboured for her? Was their subtle romance some illusion that his mind had spun as he fell head over heels in love with her? Could it all have been naught but a a figment of his imagination?

Unable to continue to lie in bed and drive himself mad, Peter finally tore the thick linen blanket away from him and seated himself in front of the desk in his room. Pulling out the complimentary stationery from its drawer, he began composing a fervently-penned letter bound for Wellington Manor.

Chapter Fourteen

Happy Black Friday (in my timezone at least)!

"A LETTER FOR YOU, MY LORD." THE SERVANT BOWED AND HANDED THE young earl an intricately designed envelope identical to the one he had previously received when he was invited to the palace ball alongside his sister. His sister...he felt a headache brewing even thinking of her. He loved her so, and it pained him to maintain such a coldness against her, but the thought of her marrying his best friend felt wrong for reasons he could not articulate even to himself. He sighed before catching sight of another similar envelope in the stack.

Pointing to it, he asked, "Is that for Lady Emmeline?"

"Yes, my lord," the servant confirmed. "Is there anything else you require, my lord? If not, I will be delivering Lady Emmeline her letters—"

"That will be unnecessary," Emmett said. "Spare yourself the trouble and give them to me. I will hand them to her."

"Are you certain, my lord? It is no trouble—"

"Give them to me," Emmett repeated, his clipped tone a clear indication that he was absolutely steadfast in his stand. He wished to make amends with his sister, but was all too aware that she was avoiding him. He would need a reason to speak to her, and having possession of her mail seemed like an adequate one. She would, after all, not be able to decline receiving her correspondence.

"As you wish, my lord." The servant, forced to oblige, handed him the two envelopes, one from the palace and one not. Who else could have written her, I wonder? Emmett thought, and after the servant had gone, he carelessly turned the other letter over in his hand – only to see his sister's name in Peter Jamison's hand.

All thoughts of reconciliation temporarily departed from his mind. The captain was usually an easygoing character. Why was he, this time, so insistent upon pursuing Emmeline, despite the fierce warning previously issued? Emmett's anger bubbled from his gut to his throat, and was released in a frightening roar. In a fit of rage, he hurled the letter into the bottom drawer of his desk and locked it. It would never see the light of day again. His sister would never see it, never read its contents, never even know of its existence.

A glance at his sister's other piece of correspondence prompted him to calm himself. Picking up the fancy envelope, Emmett left his study in search of her. His first instinct was to try looking in the garden, but she was not there. Upon his return indoors, he knew exactly where to look when he heard the deep tones of the violoncello ricocheting in the hallways.

As he had anticipated, he found Emmeline Lockhart in the music room, with her maid in waiting standing in the corner and observing her. The young lady, entranced by her instrument, did not notice him push the door open; but Penelope lifted her head and bobbed a curtsy. He nodded curtly before standing by the door and watching his sister play with naught but tenderness in his eyes. He knew how much she loved the violoncello, and there was something in the way in which she could cradle the fingerboard in her arm like a tender babe that warmed his being. As her brother and guardian, he could never stop her from doing what she loved, and her heart lay in the oversized violin that sat in her lap.

When the song Emmeline was playing drew to a close, she lifted her head to greet him, her voice soft and sad. "Emmett."

"I have a letter for you," he announced, "from the palace. I imagine it is an invitation of some sort, for I received one also."

She said nothing, as if at a loss for words, and it broke his heart that his typically smart-mouthed sister had nothing left to say to him. "I need to speak with you, Emmeline." With a glance at Penny, he added, "In private."

The young maid looked to her mistress for permission to leave. Emmeline hesitated for a split second, but eventually nodded, and she excused herself. Now brother and sister were in the same room, feeling quite estranged, and Emmett found that he hated himself for causing what could very well be the ruination of their twenty-year relationship. He only hoped that she would speak to him.

"I must apologise," he said when the door closed behind Penny, "sincerely. Emmeline, I regret being so harsh with you more than anything I have ever been sorry for in my life. I suppose I felt unhappy with the fact that you would so outrightly disobey me but...you must understand that I was only looking after your interests. Emmeline—Linnie—promise me you will not speak to him again."

"Emmett, how can you make me choose so?"

"Promise me."

"I cannot, and least not immediately."

Emmett sighed, but handed her her letter. "This is from the castle. I imagine Aunt Bethany will bring it up at dinner." With that, he left the room without a goodbye. His footsteps echoed behind him, and as he wrenched the door open, Penny stumbled in. Thankfully, he said nothing of it, and proceeded back to his study with a trail of coldness in his wake.

***

DINNER WAS, AS EMMETT HAD ANTICIPATED, FILLED WITH BETHANY'S words of praise and appreciation for the Queen's outstanding graciousness. As the marchioness claimed, at least, Sarah had taken many pains to, at very late notice, obtain three exclusive invitations to the King's annual dinner gala, where all the dukes and duchesses in the country would be assembled for a night of food and dancing. It would, Bethany said, be a good opportunity for Emmett to begin to find a wife (or rather, to seek a father-in-law), and an excellent chance for Emmeline to work towards securing her own marriage. William, Bethany, Emmett and Emmeline were to proceed to St James' Palace for the event the next day. The young lady Emmeline made a valiant attempt to smile courteously at her aunt, but could muster only what felt like a pained grimace. She found herself quite dreading having to attend another royal event: over all their meetings, Sarah had quite lost her mystic nature in her eyes. The queen, although admittedly terribly kind to her, was ultimately just another woman who wanted her to marry a man she did not love.

After the meal, Emmeline turned to find Penelope missing. She frowned, but said nothing aloud of it, and when the time came, she curtsied to her father and to her aunt and retreated to her chambers alone. Her maid-in-waiting was missing there too, and unable to undress for bed alone, the young lady pulled out a book from her trunk, sat, and waited patiently. She was not angry with the girl, since she was not in any mad rush to turn in for the night; although she did find herself rather curious as to where the young girl had disappeared away to, and what had caused her to abandon her duties so. Penny had always been diligent and dutiful, and was never the kind to be absent from the places she was supposed to be at without an extremely valid reason.

It was not long before Emmeline could receive the answers she sought. The service door flew open so abruptly that she jumped in her seat, and Penny scampered in, quite out of breath and an sheet of white letter paper clutched tightly in her hands. "Oh—my lady!"

Having recovered from her shock, Emmeline raised her eyebrows with mild amusement. "Goodness me, are you quite all right? You look like you have been standing out in the wind without your cloak."

"Oh, my lady, never mind my appearance for now! There is something far more important to do." The girl's demeanour remained completely serious, but this only drew a laugh from her mistress.

"Do you mean getting ready for bed, by any chance?"

"No," she replied, saying nothing else and instead simply thrusting the letter in her hands towards Emmeline. The whiteness of her knuckles contrasted starkly against the rosy hue of her cheeks, and the paper was crumpled beyond belief. Only raising an eyebrow at the maid's suspicious behaviour, the young lady accepted the letter and turned it over to read.

If her relationship with her brother had not been ruined before, it must have been ruined now.

The message was written in the spidery handwriting she knew and loved, but its contents were filled with unbelievable amounts of venom and rattled her like she had never been shaken before.

Peter

I cannot begin to express my disappointment ... I have told you very clearly that you should not be courting my sister, warned you against it in the most explicit terms, and you have chosen to ignore me. I thought you might want to be informed that I found the letter for her you send to my father's residence. She will not be receiving it.

I believed her and I trusted you. I truly was under the impression that you were not seeing each other. Yet, if you were not in contact, how else would you know that she is in London, staying in my father's home? And what on earth are you doing in London, Peter, staying so near the palace? Do you take me for an idiot? I was always better than you at arithmetic. It was easy for me to connect the dots. You are here pursuing her. You must have been to every dance she attended on invitation from the Queen, yes? You must have been working so hard to charm her – for she is so smitten with you. My sister is usually clever and independent, and takes my advice most seriously, but she dissolves to putty in your hands.

Peter, I have said it before and I will say it again. It is deeply unsettling for me that you and my sister might be together. Before we lose our friendship altogether I beseech you think from my point of view – I pray you think for your dearest friend. Perhaps I should not have used threats from the beginning. If you listen now it might not be too late to salvage our friend-ship. I will explain it to you – if she marries you, if she boards a ship with you and leaves me, I will be left with nothing. I shall not have my dearest friend nor my dearest sister. I will be more alone than I have ever been in my life and you may call me selfish but I cannot let her leave me for you.

I will apologise, but I cannot compromise on my stand. I am sorry. You may choose any woman for a wife but Emmeline. She means too much to me. I hope you will come to your senses sooner than later – if you still choose not to, I will offer no more apology for my response to your decision, whatever that may be.

Best wishesEmmett Lockhart

His motives were clear now. Clearly, his arguments about her emotional wellbeing had only been a guise for securing his selfish ends...but he did make a valid case. If she married Peter, the alternative to perpetually waiting for her husband to come home would be to travel with him. Penelope had mentioned this before, and it was clear now that Emmett had thought of it as well. Emmeline was torn. She never did realise that marrying the man she loved would harm her brother – her confidant, supporter, friend, and only family. The mere thought of hurting him so caused her heartache. And yet the very notion of marrying anyone but Peter Jamison made her feel hollow inside. Once again, it had all come down to the choice she had to make, the choice that would decide – and potentially ruin – the rest of her life. How could she marry a man she did not love? Simultaneously, how could she let her brother down?

The necessity, however, for her to look after Emmett's feelings began to seem questionable to her. After all, he had been so willing to forsake her happiness for his own. Why should she not choose to do the same? Because she loved him? But did he not love her?... Did he truly love her? Had her entire life been a lie and an illusion?

The young lady's head began to ache with questions. A gentle hand on her forearm prompted her to look up, and be met my Penny's sympathetic gaze. "I am sorry, my lady. Perhaps my retrieval of the letter was a mistake...I thought it would make things easier for you to understand, but—"

Emmeline chuckled humourlessly. "No. None of this is your fault."

"Would you like to go to bed now, my lady? Perhaps some rest would do you well."

"I do not think I would be able to sleep."

"Shall I remain with you?"

"Pray do so," Emmeline murmured, before gesturing towards the chair opposite hers. "Sit."

The maid complied, and the duo sat in silence for a while before she spoke again.

"My lady, His Lordship wrote that Captain Jamison sent you a letter... Where has he hidden it, I wonder?"

"Oh, Penny." She sighed. "I am not certain I wish to know."

***

MY DEAREST EMMELINE

I cannot seem to stop thinking of you in your navy gown... And this question has been burning in my heart for far too long. I saw you dancing with His Highness Prince Alexander – does he have your heart? If he does not, might I be so bold as to ask if I do?

I am a seaman, Emmeline, and you know this: I am not one for poetry or romance, but I can only write you my truest sentiments – in two visits and six dances you have captured my heart. I have fallen in love with you. Truly, madly, deeply, and most irreversibly. Every breath I breathe is occupied by thoughts of you so much that my head aches. The thought of going on a ship and being away from you pains me like no other. The thought of spending my life without you pains me like no other...and I intended to ask you this in a more romantic setting, but I cannot suppress my affections for you any further. I swear to the Lord above that I love you more than I have loved any woman before.

Will you marry me?

Please write me, my love. I beg you, for the anticipation will tear me apart.

With lovePeter

Chapter Fifteen

EMMELINE HAD NOT SAID A WORD TO EMMETT SINCE SHE HAD READ HIS letter to Peter. She thought it might have been imprudent to confront him before the dinner at the palace, in case it would affect his mood drastically when he was making such a public appearance and had some negative repercussion on the good things associated with his name. She would have her word with him the day after. She dreaded speaking to him about what he had written to Peter, for despite what she hoped, she knew that it would not end prettily.

At the gala, Emmeline found herself wedged between her father and aunt, once again in the King's dining room. She was relieved to, at least, not be seated next to her brother; but the tensions between them were sky high, although Bethany, who sat between the siblings, did not seem to sense it at all. Despite all her circumstances, Emmeline attempted to find some cheer in the food she knew would have the chance to enjoy once the meal began. From experience, she knew that King Andrew was not a stingy man when he hosted a meal.

The table was loud with chatter. Some of the noblemen at the table had not seen one another for a long time due to issues with proximity between lands, and it was the common sentiment of all the dukes that there was much to be said. Emmeline, who had never seen her own father in such a setting before, found him speaking quite amicably with the Duke of Westchester. He seemed so bitter and isolated to her that she, in all honesty, had never expected that he would have any friends at all.

The King himself, seated at the head of the table, was engaged in a grave conversation with the crown prince Alexander, whose defiant expression betrayed that he was as unhappy with his father as ever. Then King Andrew simply brushed him off and tapped his fork against his glass to demand attention. A hush came over the table, and satisfied, he spoke with his thunderous voice.

"I believe you have all heard of my son's imminent marriage, and I have had many of you suggest your daughters as his future wife and as our future queen. I thank you all for your generous offers, but we can only choose one lady," he said. Emmeline tensed, praying over and over in her mind that it would not be her, that they had found a more suitable candidate. Bethany, on the other hand, shook with anticipation, praying over and over that her niece would be chosen, for she knew that there was not a single more suitable candidate.

"Sarah and I have come to a decision, and we have chosen to announce it tonight," he declared. A light anticipatory buzz filled the room. "My wife will do the honours."

"My lords and my ladies, I am so happy to share with you today that we have selected Emmeline Lockhart of Portsmouth." The queen beamed at the young woman as her life crumbled before her eyes, the grand institution of dignity and freedom she had built over twenty-three years falling away from her reality like rain in a thunderstorm. "This is a joint decision by my husband, my son—"

There was a loud bang. Alexander had chosen this moment to slam his hand against the table and rise from his seat, his hands trembling with indignation and rage. "This was by no means a joint decision!"

"Alexander, what exactly do you think you are doing?" King Andrew hissed, his voice low and threatening. "Be seated right this instant!"

"No!" Alexander shouted, the single word echoing in the high ceiling of the dining hall. "Mother, you may announce all you like that you want that shameless, pretentious woman to marry me, but you will never be able to force me to take her as my wife! I hate her, and I hate you!"

With that, he bowed in the most demeaning way Emmeline had ever seen anyone bow, and stormed out of the room, leaving the thunders of his irate footsteps ricocheting in his wake.

There was an awkward silence shrouding the table. Finally the King cleared his throat. "I apologise for his behaviour, but let us not let him spoil our fun. He will be persuaded in due course, for Lady Emmeline is indeed a lovely maiden. But come, everyone, let us begin our meal in celebration of the prosperous year that we have seen."

Everyone nodded and grunted their agreement, and the volume of the chatter was just starting to rise again when Emmeline stood from her chair. Then it was silent, and all eyes were on her. She offered an awkward smile and curtsied for good measure before moving to stand before the monarchs at the head of the table. "If I may seek your pardon, Your Majesties... I must go to speak with His Highness."

"It is kind of you to offer to persuade him to be reasonable about this, my dear, but I must advise you not to take the pains to talk sense into that boy," Sarah said with a heavy sigh. "He cannot be convinced to think rationally.

You know, he has always been terribly rash. Occasionally I doubt that he has any good sense in that head of his."

"I must concur with her," Andrew agreed with a resigned nod. "My son has everything but a level head. I appreciate the sentiment behind your offer, Lady Emmeline, but it is no use."

"No, Your Majesties," Emmeline protested. "I must speak with him... There are things he must know before he decides his reaction to this matter."

Andrew eyed her with a creased brow, trying to look into the girl's soul and understand her motives. Yet he could see no black-hearted aim she could have in seeking to provide his son with counsel, and thus he eventually nodded with a sigh. "Then go. Have one of the servants take you to his chambers. Ask for privacy if you need it."

Emmeline nodded with a grateful smile and dropped a curtsy to both the rulers and the noblemen in the room before hurrying out. She caught a palace guard milling about outside the dining hall and requested his assistance. Albeit slightly surprised at what the palace guest asked of him, given the prince's current mood, he seemed content to comply, and led her through the winding halls and up quite a few flights of stairs.

"Here it is, my lady," the guard announced when they arrived outside a door, large and brown like every other door Emmeline had seen in the castle, perhaps even plainer than the rest. She had expected some special detailing or perhaps a plaque declaring that that room was where the His Royal Highness the Crown Prince Alexander slept, but there was none. "Would you like me to wait outside for you?"

"No, thank you, Sir," she replied, curtsying slightly. "I imagine I shall be able to find my own way back to the dining hall."

The guard bowed and took his leave. Taking a calming breath, Emmeline raised her fist and rapped on the door.

"How many times must I tell you that I have no desire to eat?" There was no movement from inside the room that she could detect, but Alexander's voice responded in an irate roar. She might have jumped if she had not already been expecting him to be so maddened.

"I do not intend to coerce you to return to dinner, Your Highness," she replied in her clearest, loudest voice. She wrung her hands subconsciously, hoping that she would not further enrage the Prince.

"I have no desire to see you either, Lady Emmeline."

"May I come in? I need to speak with you."

There was a long silence before he finally answered. "What do you wish to speak about?"

"I must make my intentions known."

"... Very well. Come in."

Emmeline pushed the door open and slipped inside the room, where she saw a garment she recognised as Prince Alexander's jacket lying discarded on the floor. She paused to shut the door behind her. Then, with some hesitation, she stepped further into the dark room.

The prince must not have bothered to light any lamps. He was sitting in a sofa before a window, clearly brooding. What remained of the day's sunlight fell in half-hearted beams through the glass, accentuating all his troubled features. His brow was furrowed, his eyes without a hint of joy. His lips were softly downturned, and Emmeline thought that he himself must not know that he was frowning. She felt a pang of sympathy in her heart for this unhappy man. What a life a prince must lead for him to be so sad...

"Your Highness," she greeted, her voice quiet. "I apologise. I should have spoken to you about this sooner, but I could never find the chance."

"Sit," he said with a sigh, gesturing to the opposite end of the sofa. After she had lowered herself onto the plush seat, he asked, "How much?"

The sudden question caught Emmeline off-guard, and with a brow furrowed in confusion, she blurted out, "What?"

"How much money do you want? How much do I have to pay you to leave me in peace?"

"Your Highness, you must know how I feel about—"

"Dear Lord, if you tell me you are madly in love with me, I—"

"There is a man I care for!" Emmeline suddenly heard herself shouting, cutting the prince off before he could begin to insult her based on a groundless assumption he had made. "With all due respect, Your Highness, I must remind you that I hardly know you, and that during our few interactions, there has been no kindness to speak of on your part. If I may be so bold to be candid with you, it really is quite preposterous that you would assume that man would be you."

Alexander remained wordless, and it was for such a long time that Emmeline wondered if she should simply leave. Perhaps he would never answer. Perhaps he was offended at her calling him unkind. Upsetting the crown prince was undesirable, to say the least, but Emmeline found herself caring less and less about it.

"Then why are you now engaged to me?" he finally asked, and she was almost surprised that he had said anything at all.

"My Aunt Bethany arranged this," she explained. "Before I was first sent to meet you, I tried to tell her about Captain Jamison... She asked me if I loved him. I could not lie to her. Then, I did not...and so she sent me here. Merely because I did not love him yet, she believed I would love you." She sighed. "I mean no offence, Your Highness, but you have not been particularly amiable, and I tried to tell her that I do not wish to be wed to you. Unfortunately, that only gained me a lesson on resilience."

"Captain Jamison?" Alexander echoed, turning to look at her. He did not seem to be very interested in her plight, instead choosing to ask after the man she had mentioned, "Your lover is a naval officer, then?"

"Yes," she confirmed, avoiding his gaze as she felt her cheeks heat up, "but he is not my lover, Your Highness, you make it sound scandalous. He is also one of the most agreeable, polite and respectful gentlemen I have ever met."

The prince smiled, but it did not touch his eyes. "Very good, Lady Emmeline. I will bring this information to my parents. We will not marry. You will have your Captain and I shall rule without a queen." He paused. "I am glad that we discussed this."

Emmeline met his eyes now, and allowed herself to give out one of her rare grins. He did not seem quite so unpleasant now. "You know, Your Highness, you seem to have the same aversion to marriage as my brother does."

"I suppose there is at least one individual in this palace who shares my views." He chuckled. "Does your father too have a maiden he wishes him to marry?"

"There is a Lady Adelaide Farthingale," Emmeline replied thoughtfully. "But I do not think the match will be very successful, for she is far too lively.

If my brother's rejection of her fails to persuade my father, I will veto it myself."

Alexander smiled at her. "You are quite likeable, Emmeline, and I think we might one day be dear friends, but I doubt I shall ever wish to marry you."

Emmeline laughed. "I doubt I shall ever wish to marry you, either."

***

QUEEN SARAH'S FACE LIT UP WHEN SHE SAW EMMELINE LOCKHART WALK into the dining hall again on her son's arm. No one had ever managed to cajole Alexander into returning to a meal or party after he had had an angry fit before, and to her it was only a sign that the girl was very suited to be his new wife. The King seemed equally surprised, but neither monarch paid any comment. The noblemen and noblewomen began to murmur with intrigue and how Emmeline Lockhart seemed to have tamed his temper.

Even as her heart broke for the grief that was likely to befall the queen, the young lady swept into a curtsy in greeting, and the prince offered a curt bow.

"Father, Mother," Alexander addressed the monarchs with more gravity than his parents had ever heard him speak with. "Lady Emmeline and I have discussed our situation, and we have come to a consensus."

"Yes, son," Sarah prompted, her eyes dancing with anticipation.

"Emmeline and I have come to be rather fond of one another," he announced. "It is our common opinion, however, that marriage would only bring ruin to all friendly sentiment we have found for each other, and it would be a capital shame to forsake such a friendship. As such, I should refuse to marry her, and I believe she will reject me as a husband with equal conviction. I will rule without a queen."

Emmeline's eyes widened in horror. Why does he deliver such news thus impertinently? she screamed inwardly, it is as if he worries he will not upset Sarah sufficiently! As much as she wished to speak her mind out loud, it was hardly her place to rebuke the prince, and so she said nothing. The room was deathly silent for a long while. All the nobility in the room seemed frozen, shocked by his impudence. Emmeline clutched her left hand in her right, on the verge of swooning. Emmett looked quite alarmed, eyes wide. Alexander smiled quite smugly, looking as if he had just accomplished something great. Sarah, however, looked completely crestfallen, and King Andrew's stern eyes were trained on his son in a livid glare. Then the suffocating motionlessness of the room vanished all at once as Sarah rose abruptly, shaky on her usually strong legs, and all but ran out of the room, quite flustered, with a hand over her mouth.

"My lords; my ladies. If you would excuse yourselves... There will be service in the ballroom shortly. Wait staff, ensure that the guests are attended to."

All the visitors and most of servants evacuated the room with more immediacy than Emmeline had ever seen nobility take action, tittering nervously.

Then, when the room had been cleared and the sound of people's talk gone, the King's hand came down harshly upon the dining table. The plates upon it clattered noisily in response as if in shock. Emmeline shrunk further into her thin frame. The servants present fled the room. Only Alexander seemed unperturbed, his blue eyes looking more alive than ever. Andrew seemed to suddenly notice the young lady standing by his son, quite terrified.

"Lady Emmeline... I apologise, but I shall have to invite you to proceed to the ballroom as well. There are some...matters I must discuss with my son in private." His voice was far too quiet, and it warned of a thunderous storm to come. Emmeline nodded, curtsied and left the room as calmly as she could, uttering a prayer for Alexander. She knew that he was, despite all that he had said, not a bad person, only an insensitive and brash one. He did not deserve much of the ill fortune that could befall him should he continue to fail to speak sensibly to his father in this situation. Yet there was nothing she could do for him now but hope for the best.

"See what you have done!" the King bellowed the moment the Portsmouth girl's footsteps died out. "You have made your mother cry – is that what you wish to see?"

"No," Alexander replied calmly. "All I have ever wished for is to make a choice for myself. For, perhaps, the first time in my life, I have done that today, and I refuse to admit shame or regret for it. In fact, I will say that I feel extraordinarily liberated."

"The cheek of you, you good-for-nothing fool!" Andrew thundered, standing with such force that his chair overturned behind him, landing on the floor with a crash. "You are not fit to be King!"

"And you are not fit to be a father. Both you and Mother would sell my happiness for power in a heart—"

"How dare you!" Andrew roared. "Very well. Since you are thus intent on causing your own damnation...since you refuse to grow out of your childish, self-centred ways, I have no choice left!"

Then he turned away from the rebellious prince, and his voice became scarily quiet as quickly as it had risen to ear-shattering volumes.

"You will marry Emmeline Lockhart within the year... Or I will give your place as King to your cousin George."

Prince Alexander only scoffed at the ultimatum. "You know I have never had any desire to be King, Father. You can let George have the throne for all I care!"

"Foolish child, you try my patience." Andrew's voice was ice cold as he uttered the most unfeeling words Emmeline had ever heard. "Do you truly believe that I, a King who would do anything for the wellbeing of his country, would be reluctant to go as far as to exile you if you continue to force my hand in this way?"

"Father... You would not."

"Would I not?" he countered. "You know this, son. I love my country, and I love your mother. I will defend both to the death, regardless of what it requires me to do. If you leave me with no choice, I will banish you from the kingdom."

Alexander would never admit this to anyone, but his eyes sparkled with sadness. "You say you love this country and you love Mother... Tell me, Father, do you not love me?"

"You are the offensive party in this situation, Alexander."

"Answer the question!"

"Alexander..."

"Do you love me, or do you not?"

"With your rebellious ways and your impertinent behaviour... You have given me no cause to."

The prideful prince swallowed the pained scream that battled to be let out of his throat. He stood silent and ramrod straight as the man he wished he could call his father walked past him on his way out of the room without another word. When the King's footsteps finally faded from earshot, he sunk to his knees, and, in the middle of the dining hall, began to shake with not the blind rage that guided the King, but the grief of a child unloved.

Chapter Sixteen

THE CARRIAGE RIDE BACK TO WELLINGTON HOUSE WAS A SILENT ONE. Emmeline had tears in her eyes the whole time as she thought of what was to become of her when she married Prince Alexander, and what was to become of her relationship with the handsome Captain who had quite captured her affections. It must have been too dark for Emmett to notice, for he said nothing of it. Emmeline longed for him to say something, but she had never been the kind of woman to beg for attention from others. To her, it was most unbecoming and most unladylike, for Miss Paltrow had taught her that ladies never expressed grief so openly unless the occasion called for it. She was not about to becoming a simpering chit. Besides, her relationship with Emmett was far less than stellar at that moment, and so she simply stayed mute and tried to keep her breathing steady and light until they finally arrived at the gates of her father's property.

Once the carriage had ground to a stop, William left the party without a word, presumably walking towards his chambers. Quite used to his rudeness, no one of the remaining three commented on his abrupt departure.

"Well, I truly am exhausted," Emmett sighed. "I will retire now. Goodnight."

"Yes – goodnight, my dear," Bethany responded. "What theatrics the prince put up! I am quite drained myself. Goodnight, everyone."

Willing her voice not to waver, she said, as clearly as she could, "Goodnight."

Bethany and Emmett vanished from her vicinity. Bathed in semi-darkness and alone at last, Emmeline exhaled deeply and closed her eyes, allowing a tear to escape her eyelid and streak down her powdered cheek. Then, hastily daubing it away with her embroidered handkerchief, she took a calming breath and started most determinedly for her room, where Penelope had said she would be waiting.

"Emmeline."

Her father's voice stopped her short in her tracks, and she turned, albeit reluctantly, to see him standing behind her with a glowing lamp in his hand. The orange luminescence that touched his face in the otherwise shadowed area made him look gentler than she had ever seen him. His eyes, for the first time in Emmeline's life, did not display a lack of love, but betrayed the hurt buried deep in the greying man's soul, the heartbreak that surfaced now at the sight of his daughter in tears.

"Yes, Father?" Determined to salvage whatever dignity she had left, Emmeline straightened and furiously blinked back all remaining tears in her eyes.

"Come," he said, his voice uncharacteristically kind, "sit with me in the library, my dear. I need to speak with you."

Emmeline was puzzled, exhausted, and wanted to be left alone to grieve the loss of her own life, but complied without a word of complaint, instead trailing silently behind her father as he walked to the single room his house he had some degree of fondness for. The library was well-lit by the crystal chandelier it boasted, and William snuffed the flame of his lamp. He seated himself in his armchair near the hearth in the heart of the room and gestured for his daughter to sit opposite him. With a short curtsy, she obeyed.

"Emmeline," he sighed, "you must know...I am very sorry."

"Why do you apologise?" she asked, bewildered. Her father had never apologised to her nor her brother in the entirety of their lives; what motivated him to do so now? Was it too late to offer any apology for the death of her mother? Why would he only seek her forgiveness now when she was already an adult about to be married? What had prompted his sudden sentiment of guilt? Was it her marriage?

"There is much that you do not understand, my dear," he replied with a tight smile. "And, despite what he thinks, there is little that your brother truly knows about me, and about what happened with your mother all those years ago. He thinks he remembers, but he was such a wee child, hardly an infant, and you know you do not recall what had happened. Perhaps the two of you never will know me as I wish you would...but, Emmeline, I did not call you here to listen to me complain. All I ask is that you bear this in mind."

Emmeline prompted elaboration with anticipatory silence, and William continued. "I love you, Emmeline, very much. Both you and your brother. I would do anything for the pair of you...I would give my life. I know you think I do not because of the series of events with your mother, and even with Countess Riddell." He stopped for a while, swallowing. Emmeline felt her heart soften. "You know, I could not love her – for Anne – in the way a husband should love a wife, and there were times when I could not stand to look at her for the things she reminded me of, but I cared for her nonetheless... I grieved her passing almost as much as you did."

The last sentence that left William's lips incurred an steely anger deep within the chambers of Emmeline's heart that had faded over the years. She remembered all that Emmett had told her – Father made Mother cry,

Mother died because of Father, Father could hardly wait to be rid of her. While William seemed to make a case that might very well be valid and true, the words her older brother had spoken to her in their childhood remained gospel in her heart. Looking at the aged man before her, she still found it difficult to believe him.

"Why are you telling me this now?" she demanded. "Emmett and I may not share a very harmonious relationship at the present moment, but that hardly means I will listen blindly to whatever you wish to tell me."

"My dear, Emmett is sorely mistaken." William sighed. "I see that you remain his ardent supporter, regardless of what he has done to you. Very well." He turned in search of his butler, and spotted him in the far corner of the room, standing there in case his employer required anything of him. "Collins? Please send for my son."

"Yes, Your Grace. Immediately." The butler rushed out of the room. Emmeline sat with her brow furrowed, trying to make sense of the entire situation. She wished she could just return to being the carefree Lady Emmeline of Portsmouth who spent all her time riding with her brother and playing the violoncello instead of worrying about being married off to the crown prince and brooding over being separated from the man she loved and getting involved in arguments with her distant father. She just wished it could all go back to normal. She just wanted her life with her brother back—

...regardless of what he has done to you...

Standing suddenly, she trained a pair of hawk-like eyes at William, attempting to search his soul through its windows. Her voice came out stiffly – and almost mechanically – as she posed the question on her mind, the question she had not thought to think of even once when she moved away from her father and lived her life without him. She had always assumed that he was naught but a stranger she simply happened to have blood ties to – she had always assumed that he was uninformed of who his daughter had matured to be, of the people she had grown to love and of all the other goings-on in her life…

"Father, what do you know?"

William met her gaze, and with a sad smile, he gave her the answer she did not want. "Everything."

***

EMMELINE HAD NOT ORIGINALLY WISHED TO BELIEVE HER FATHER, BUT he proved sufficiently within the next few hours that he did indeed know everything.

He knew about the Captain's visits and he knew about his fast friendship with Emmeline. He knew about her growing affection towards the young officer. He knew about the letters Emmett wrote, but more than that, he knew about his motives. This in particular was a heatedly-discussed subject that evening.

When the young earl walked into the room, Emmeline and William had already discussed him. He found his father reclined in his armchair, and his sister standing before the flames of the fireplace, seemingly entranced by their dance. He frowned. "Whatever could you want to speak about at this ungodly hour, Father?"

William nodded. "I was hoping—"

"Actually, Father," Emmeline interrupted, turning from the fireplace to look at her brother, "I would be greatly obliged if you would let me speak to Emmett first."

"Very well," William said. "Would you like me to leave you?"

"No, thank you," she said, her tone clipped.

Emmett's brow furrowed at the unfamiliar sharpness of her voice. "Emmeline, you sound unlike yourself this evening."

"I sound unlike myself?" she repeated. "I find that amusing, brother, for you too have been terribly unlike yourself in the past few weeks. Will you extrapolate my meaning, or do you wish me to spell it out for you?"

"Linnie, you know why I warned you against Peter—"

"Enough said, Emmett. You have made your choice clear." She turned to the butler, who had returned to his original position once he had escorted Emmett into the library. "Mr Collins? Would you be so kind as to run to Penelope, and request her presence in the library? Do ask that she brings the letter with her." As the poor butler was made to run out of the library again, she called out a "thank you" after him.

"While we wait," she said, "I believe Father has a few myths to dispel."

"Children," William sighed, "I would like to begin with an apology."

Emmeline's eyebrows rose in alarm and protest. "But Father—!"

"Listen to me, Emmeline," was his calm response, raising a hand to quiet her. "I am sorry that I was unable to support you in your earliest years. Truly, I am; but I would like to beg of you an opportunity to explain myself."

When the twins said nothing, he assumed consent and made his elaboration, finally speaking the words that he had kept in his soul under lock and eye for decades. The words he had wanted to say for so long...the words he never found the right time for. William felt uneasy. Perhaps it was still not the right time; but then, he thought, perhaps the right time would never come.

"It is true that your mother and I were not happy in our marriage – it is true that I could not love her as she deserved to be loved. It is true that we were distanced from each other...and Emmett, I understand your reasons for believing so, or wanting to believe so, but I did not grieve her to death – Anne passed away due to a combination of a twin birth and the coldest winter London had seen in many years.

"She and I were not in love, but I cared for her in a different way. Believe what you may choose to, but I did. And the two of you...you have inherited my hair, but eyes that are exactly like hers. I could not look at you without thinking of the woman I was unable to love...the woman whom I felt like I had let down. Despite what you might think, I carried the weight of her death on my shoulders. What you believe...I believed too, to some extent. I believed that it was my fault that she could not spend her last years in joy. Each time I saw you I was reminded of that thought, and on retrospect I regret it deeply, but it was because of this reason that I came to avoid you. You grew, and I knew that the two of you had developed a hatred towards me I could not redeem myself of. I did not know what to do...so I did nothing. I loved you, and I still do, but after the incident with Countess Riddell I let you leave. It felt hopeless, so I decided to let you find happiness away from me. I knew you were both fond of him, so I left you in Adalberto's care, with Penelope to keep an extra eye on Emmeline. Penelope tells Adalberto what she knows, and I receive reports from Adalberto frequently."

"What—Penny?" Emmeline exclaimed, eyes wide as saucers. "She was your informant?"

A ghost of a smile came onto the duke's lips. He nodded towards the girl who had slipped into the room mid-story and gone to stand beside Collins. "There she is; you may verify the veracity of my statement with her."

She whirled around to face her maid-in-waiting, who blushed and nodded sheepishly. "It is true, my lady. His Grace has always been concerned for you, but I was under strict instructions not to show any sign of being acquainted with him. He only ever wanted you to be happy, my lady...as I did."

William, with hopeful eyes, turned to his son, who had remained silent the whole time. "Emmett... Will you not say anything?"

He swallowed, raising his eyes to face his father and his sister – the two people whom he had done the most wrong to in all of his life, and yet the very same two of all he knew who had loved him the most. "Well, Father—Emmeline... I imagine I too have my share of apologies to make."

Thanks for reading! As usual, do vote, comment, and share! :)

Chapter Seventeen

WHAT IS A CHILD TO DO WHEN HIS MOTHER DIES?

What is a child to do when he loses the guiding beacon of his life?

What is a child to do when he wakes to find himself with nothing left?

Emmett Lockhart was woken in the middle of one night – a still, hot night – when he was only ten and two, only a boy. His arm was being shaken violently, but he could not tell if it was that or the sound of Emmeline's cries that had woken him first. The first thing he saw was his twin sister in tears, her face contorted in panic and pain. She was still in her nightgown, her hair left down and hanging down her back. The grogginess vanished from his eyes as he scrambled to sit up in bed, an ominous sense of foreboding capturing his heart.

"What happened, Linnie? What has upset you so?" Although he would be a source of comfort for Emmeline, he too had flown into something of a panic.

"It's... It's Mama," she answered between sobs. "Emmy, what do we do?"

"Mama?" His eyes grew wide, and though he had not thought it possible, his heart began to beat even faster in his breath. Their mother had been sick for some time now, complaining of severe pains in her chest. He had a feeling that he understood his sister's intonations completely, but the truth was not one that he wanted to hear. Despite his sensibility, he asked her: "Is Mama in pain again?"

Emmeline shook her head violently, untied black hair sticking to her tear-stained face. She pushed it sloppily out of the way with the heels of her palms as she struggled to form a coherent sentence in her unstable emotional state. "N-no...she... Emmy, she..." But she could not bring the words to leave her mouth, as if they would make the situation all the more real, and she burst into tears once again.

"Father... Where is Father?"

"In...the...l-l-library." Emmeline managed to respond between sobs. "Th-the d-door is l-l-locked. H-he...He w-w-won't...s-see me. Em-Emmett, I'm...I'm scared."

"I...I need to see her," he choked out, pushing himself off his bed and sliding his feet into his slippers. He was about to run straight to his mother's chambers, but his sister's hand catching onto his arm stopped him. He turned to look at her, tears still streaming down her face, naught but fear in her eyes.

"Emmy... It is – it is frightening to see her...this way."

"She's my mother, Emmeline," Emmett said determinedly. "Nothing about her could scare me."

Emmeline nodded dumbly and released her hold on him. He bolted out of the room, twisting and turning through the calls, and nearly crashed through his mother's door. The bed was covered by a white sheet, and

Anne Lockhart's maids in waiting were huddled in a corner, all in tears. They looked up in alarm upon hearing him enter.

"M-Master Emmett," one greeted. "Your mother... I'm afraid Her Grace..."

Emmett did not respond, instead rushing to his mother's bedside and pulling the sheet off her. She was so pale, her ruby lips drained of colour, her eyes shut. She could have been sleeping...if she were not so cold. Emmett rested a hand upon her face. Ice. Her life had vanished from her body... Her face was so familiar, still so comforting, but his mother was gone. His mother was gone...

Gone.

Tears sprang to Emmett's eyes, and a strangled sob emerged from his throat. He did not fight it.

His mother was gone.

She had left him.

How could she be gone?

How?

How was this possible?

She had promised she would always be there for him.

"Fret not, my child. I will always protect you."

She was gone.

Gone.

Gone.

"Always."

Gone.

Emmett Lockhart crumpled to the floor, a heap of tears and grief.

His mother was gone.

***

EMMETT WEPT FOR HOURS. BY THE TIME HE RAN OUT OF TEARS, THE SUN had risen from its grave on the horizon, crying bloody tears that stained the clouds with the agony of death. Anne's maids in waiting had stayed with him throughout the night, keeping vigil over the beautiful woman's body, but Emmeline never did seek him out. Neither, of course, did his wretched father. The thought of William Lockhart made Emmett sick with rage. If only that glacial man was kinder to her... If only his father had been a better husband, maybe his angel of a mother would still be alive. Alive to hold him, kiss him, tell he would be all right.

But she was not.

And the young boy had set his mind on the idea that there was only one man to blame for this – the one man who was supposed to be her most intimate family, the one man who would not even come to collect her body and begin arranging her memorial service.

He had grown up watching William neglect the woman he had the gall to call his wife... He had witnessed him ignoring Anne's questions about the decorations she had put up in Wellington House. He had seen his mother cry alone in her room when she thought her children were asleep, mourning her dead marriage. He had felt her tears wet on his face when he had made an attempt at offering comfort. He knew how much pain William Lockhart had put his mother through...and now she was dead. Who else was there to blame?

Eventually Emmett stood from his position by his mother. His legs ached from the stiffness of the floorboards. Seeing her face again sent a fresh wave of pain through his chest, and it was with shaking hands that he drew the sheet back over her face and whispered an "I love you".

He went in search of his sister – his poor sister. He remembered the panic on her face the night before, and while he regretted not being able to tend to her wounds, he had had his own heart to heal.

He combed Wellington House in search of her with little success. He found her where he searched last – outside the library, recoiled on the floor in a quivering ball. She was still dressed in her nightgown, her cheeks tear-stained, but perhaps what broke Emmett's heart the most was that she was asleep. How long had she been lying there, waiting for her father to lend her some kind of comfort?

Her maid in waiting sat by her, but rose hastily upon seeing the young master approach. If her expression was any indication, the servant was exhausted from spending the night without sleep.

"Good morning, Master Emmett," she greeted hastily, sweeping into a trembling curtsy. "Miss Emmeline has been here for hours. I cannot persuade her to leave – she is adamant on waiting for His Grace to emerge. Thus far, however, His Grace has refused to do see her."

Upon hearing her report this, heartache turned to rage, and he turned to the library door. He attempted to turn the doorknob, but it would not budge. Recalling what Emmeline had told him the previous night, Emmett realised that William must have locked himself inside the library upon Anne's death and not come out since. Why would he not be with his children at this time of crisis? Now that their mother had left them so permanently, the twins needed him more than ever. Did he truly not care a jot for them? Another glance at his sister enraged him enough to pound on the door and shout louder than he had ever shouted in his life.

"Father!"

"Leave me, Emmett."

"Father, I demand that you open the door!"

"Leave me."

Emmett's brow crumpled. "Your daughter has been sitting outside the library all night! How could you leave her so? Have you no heart at all?"

A pause. Then, "I said leave me, child, and take your sister with you."

He was about to shout back, angry proclamations all ready to be thrown at William on the tip of his tongue, but he was interrupted by the sound of his sister's voice. It was hoarse from all the crying she had done the previous night, and it hurt him to see her so broken.

"Emmy...?" Emmeline mumbled, stirring. She sat up. "Emmy, why are you shouting? What's happening?"

He hesitated, looking at his sister and back to the door he stood before.

Then he decided that William Lockhart was not worth upsetting her – his only close family left.

"It is nothing for you to fret over, Linnie," he said gently, moving to help her to her feet again. She was still shaking slightly, her exhaustion and depression clear not merely in the way she swayed but in the hollowness of her green eyes. The sparkle had been sapped from them, and it took effort for him to hide the way his heart clenched to see his sister so sad. "Come, now. I will escort you back to your chambers for some rest. Poor thing, you must be exhausted."

"But Emmett – I wanted to wait for Father..."

"Come, now, sister, do not be difficult. I promise you that we do not need him to still be happy. He killed our mother, Emmeline. We do not need nor want a man like him in our lives."

She paused. "I miss Mama."

"As do I, Emmeline; as do I."

***

EMMETT AND EMMELINE LOCKHART WERE NAMED AFTER THE GODDESS Leto's twin children, Apollo and Artemis. It had been Lady Anne Lockhart's wish to bless them with those middle names. She had wanted them to have all the strength of the two Greek deities; but unbeknownst to her, the twins later blossomed to resemble very much the gods they were named after.

Some said that Artemis were born first, and that she aided her mother in painlessly birthing Apollo. Although Emmett was, in truth, the older twin, Emmeline had indeed been the one to draw out his inner strength. When his mother died, his younger sister became the light of his life, the only thing worth fighting for. She had been the driving force behind the man he had made of himself. For how could he care for her if he could not be self-sufficient? It was Emmeline who spurred him to study hard, to groom himself into the best person he could be. It was Emmeline who lent him the courage to announce that he would be leaving London for Portsmouth, and taking his sister with him. It was Emmeline who encouraged him to make friends with other members of the peerage as best as he could, forming alliances both formal and informal. He had done it all for her, all in the hopes that he could give her the happy life she deserved, and the happy life he thought William had robbed her of. She meant the world to him.

This was also the reason why he could not lose her to his dearest friend.

The day Emmett Lockhart first brought his new friend Captain Peter Jamison of the Royal Navy to Lockhart Manor, he had chosen not to make any formal introductions. Peter's charisma was magnetic – it was, in fact, one of the reasons why Emmett had found himself befriending the young captain to begin with – and the young earl knew for certain that Emmeline would fall for his charms immediately. Although Emmett could not be sure that Peter would be romantically interested in his sister, he had long decided not to take any chances, for Peter's career would mean that Emmeline, if she married the navy man, might be taken from him for extended periods of time – or forever. Hence, Emmeline was not called to the drawing room while the duo enjoyed a pot of tea. The two friends did, however, pass the young lady in the hall; Emmett stopped to introduce them, and then he and Peter continued on their way to his study. A minute in each other's presence was hardly enough to generate any affections between the two, and Emmett was beyond relieved.

He remained at ease for many years, until he received a letter from his sister detailing the captain's visit to Lockhart Manor in his absence. Her words conveyed how very fond of him she was, and paranoia crawled under his skin, whispering in his ear that Jamison had taken a shine to his sister just as much.

Selfishness reared its ugly head, and Emmett, to say the least, acted unwise-ly.

He had not been not wrong in his suspicions, but Emmett would regret the choices he had made for the rest of his life.

Chapter Eighteen - Part One

H IS ROYAL HIGHNESS PRINCE ALEXANDER HAD NO MORE TEARS LEFT TO be shed. Greta had sought to see him, but he sent her away; his mother had attempted to speak to him, but he had refused; and his father – his father had made no attempt to make amends with him after their earth-shaking conflict two days ago.

Alexander's world had been plunged into one of darkness and despair, of anger and anguish. He felt furious and sad and wronged and hurt and indignant and shamed all at once, and cooped up alone in his chambers, the negativity of his thoughts had torn the fabric of his mind apart. Before he had not thought much of the world around him, but now he thought too much of it, and he hated it. He hated his country, he hated his father, he hated his mother, and he hated himself. He was on the brink of losing his mind. He did not want to marry Emmeline Lockhart, and he knew that she did not wish to be wed to him either. Yet what choice did he have in the matter? An exiled prince was as good as dead. It hurt to think of the fact that his own father had threatened him with death.

He knew that the young Lady Emmeline was equally helpless, for there was nothing else that she could do to save herself from a fate that would be just as miserable as his – a fate they would share. He would have felt sorry for her if he himself was not trapped in the same miserable plight.

He did not want to eat or drink, sleep or stand. He simply lay, his bed a coffin for his dead soul. He might as well have been dead... It would be easier, he thought, than this. And who would be there to miss him? His parents did not love him, and his country did not need him, and he knew that George would be more than willing – overjoyed, in fact – to step up to the plate and take on the name of King in his place.

With all these thoughts crowding his consciousness, Alexander was tempted to take to the bottle; but he did not want to waste his last moments of bachelorhood in a drunken stupor. And so he abstained, squandering away his last days in other ways, filling them with all the depression of the tragedy in the plays he used to enjoy.

***

WHILE ALEXANDER SAT ISOLATED IN HIS CHAMBERS, CAPTAIN PETER Jamison was out calling on a friend, and seated in Thomas Maxwell's drawing room. Yet he did not feel any better than the the other young man did – for Tom had just notified him that his lady love was engaged to the crown prince.

Peter had been telling his friend of his affections for her, professing his love a second time as if he were speaking to Emmeline herself. Then he told Tom about the unreturned letter, and of the anxieties it had driven him to. He felt like he would go mad if he did receive word from her, and with every passing day the urge to call on her at Wellington House grew stronger.

"Pray, what is her name?" Thomas asked, with a smile equal parts amused and patient. "I should like to know which fine lady has my dear friend so enchanted."

"Emmeline," was his reply, the way he spoke her name as tender as a budding flower bathed in morning dew. "Emmeline Lockhart, of Portsmouth."

At the mention of her name, Mrs Maxwell became quite alarmed, and reached out a hand to touch her husband's arm as her eyes grew wide. "Emmeline Lockhart, is she not the one whom Prince Alexander is...?"

"What is it, Diane?" Peter asked feverishly as he became infected with her panic, "What causes you such shock? What do you know of Emmeline?"

Not knowing how to deliver such terrible news to him, Diane Maxwell shifted uncomfortably. Sensing her distress, Tom was quick to rescue her and patted her hand reassuringly before taking on the task of telling Peter of the engagement himself. He smiled sympathetically at his friend, and said, "Well, you see, Peter – Diane and I were recently notified by my godmother of an engagement, between Prince Alexander and a young lady... We were informed that her name is Emmeline Lockhart."

"Engaged...to the crown prince?" Peter echoed in disbelief, collapsing back in his chair. "How could this be?" He froze, a single memory that had plagued him one night coming to mind. "I saw them dancing together. Could she have been... Was she merely toying with my emotions?"

Tom sighed. "You have my sympathies, Peter. But you must not not despair, my friend, for I assure you that there are plenty more lovely women to be had."

"Plenty to be had... But none that I am in love with, Thomas, none that I wish to have." The response was somber and defeated. "Emmeline has captured my heart...and now, with news of the engagement, she has shattered it."

Tom Maxwell's lips stretched in a grim smile as he made another attempt at comforting the captain. "If she would hurt you so, perhaps she does not love you; and, as your ardent friend, if she does not love you, she does not deserve you."

"I love her," was all Peter could respond with. He did not seem to be angry, only grieving and hurt, as he slumped backwards in his chair. Seeing the poor man so discouraged incited Diane's greatest sympathies; yet the difference between the two Maxwells was that the husband expressed sympathy with consolation, while the wife typically chose to do everything in her power to help the individual whose predicament touched her heart.

"You know, Peter," she remarked, "while Tom is correct to a certain extent, not all marriages are a matter of will." She turned to her husband. "You know I love you very much, darling, but I must disagree with you on this point. I think it would be unwise to be so quick to assume that Lady Emmeline harboured the intention of hurting him. From what I have heard of her, Lady Emmeline is a very proper, educated, charitable and kind young woman – hardly, if you ask me, the kind to toy with a good man's heart and then marry a prince."

"Diane, my love," John said in a low voice, "did you not see how happy Godmother was about it? I comprehend fully what you imply, and I understand your intentions, but I can hardly stand the thought of hurting my greatest benefactor so."

"If you do not wish to be involved in doing the right thing for two young people, my dear, then you are more than welcome to stay out of it. I respect Her Majesty for being a woman as great as she is, and I am thankful to her for all she has done for you, but her achievements certainly do not allow her to hurt others to suit her own fancies. Peter began as your friend, but he has also become mine, and I cannot sit and watch him lose the love of his life over the whim of a king." Unlike her husband, Diane spoke loudly, and the captain was fully able to hear each one of her words.

"To suit her fancies? The whim of a king?" Peter asked, looking up. His brows were knitted as he sought to understand what she proposed. As he made his enquiry, his trained mind was already decoding her words. "Whatever might you mean by that, Diane?"

Thomas sighed, seeing that he could not stop his wife despite anything he might try to say, and chose to rise from his seat. Excusing himself, he retired to his chambers. Diane did not stop him. Despite their disagreement, both of them were of the common opinion that presence would only complicate the whole affair.

"Well," she said once her husband had taken his leave, "people have been talking about the King's gala dinner, where the engagement was announced. There was quite a commotion; for the prince was rather...upset by it. And, allegedly, the His Highness and Lady Emmeline made a joint statement in front of all the dukes in the land that they are, in fact, quite in opposition of the engagement."

"Truly?" Peter's eyes were, once again, filled with hope, and they drew a smile from Diane.

"Truly," she confirmed. "What do you think you would like to do now?"

"I will speak to her, and to her father," he replied, his jaw set in determination and his voice quite resembling how it sounded when he informed his crew of his plan of action. "I will go to Wellington House and ask for her hand in marriage. I will fight Emmett if I must."

Diane did not understand the complexity of his situation, but nodded encouragingly. "Whatever happens, Peter, you have my support...and Tom's as well, I'm sure. I know he has chosen to make himself scarce this afternoon, and I know you might question his willingness to help you at the present moment, but I know him better than anyone else under the sun, and I promise that he is still your friend."

Despite everything, Peter grinned. "Thank you, Diane."

Chapter Eighteen - Part Two

- -

"P ARDON MY INTRUSION, MY LADY, BUT HIS GRACE YOUR FATHER HAS requested your presence in the drawing room immediately. There is a gentleman with him."

Gathering the skirts of her brown lace dress, Emmeline rose. "Very well. I will be there shortly," she said to the servant as he bowed and retreated from the service door. "Thank you." She turned to her maid-in-waiting, who had been busying herself with tidying the young lady's dresses and undergarments when the messenger came into the room. "Come along now, Penny."

The duo proceeded through the halls of Wellington House. Penelope opened the drawing room door for Emmeline, who glided into the room, shoulders back and hands clasped together in the way that she walked in front of strangers. It was tiring, perhaps; but Miss Paltrow thought it proper and elegant, and, despite having been independent from the governess for many years, Emmeline still followed most of her decrees by force of habit.

Her lips parted slightly in surprise when she saw her father seated in his chair, with Captain Jamison and her brother seated in the sofa beside him. She felt her head spin and quite nearly collapsed, but composed herself with a steadying breath. Despite managing to remain on her two feet, she still found herself quite unable to form words.

"Ah," William greeted with a smile, "come, my dear, sit."

The sound of a human voice rendered her suddenly able to speak, and the words in her throat seemed to battle to be let out first. Tears sprang to her eyes at the thought of the situation at hand, the sight of the wonderful man who could have been her fiancé only another reminder of her plight.

"P—Pe—Captain...!" she stuttered, her words snagging in her throat as her shimmering emerald eyes trained themselves on the dashing young man. They were seemingly blind to all else in the room, and her father's invitation to sit was long forgotten as she attempted to explain everything and apologise profusely all at once. "Oh, Captain Jamison, I—I... I didn't mean for—I tried..."

"Linnie, come and sit. All words that must be spoken will be said in due time – I promise." Emmett's voice was gentle, and as green eyes met familiar green eyes, the young lady felt a sense of safety despite her predicament. As she sat down on the other identical plush sofa, she found herself glad and relieved to have once again regained her older brother's love and support in a turbulent time like this.

"Captain Jamison is aware of the engagement," William said. Emmeline's anxiety skyrocketed immediately and she opened her mouth to speak, but her father stopped her. "Hold on just one minute, Emmeline. The captain came calling with the suspicion that you are an unwilling party, and Emmett and I have explained the situation to him."

"You will take none of the blame, Emmeline," Peter said with sadness in his hazel eyes, "you could have done nothing more."

"No, Peter, I should have been far more explicit with Aunt Bethany," she disagreed, shaking her head vehemently. "There is no one to blame but me." Saying this triggered something within her, and she felt her calm crumble completely as she broke down in a fit of tears. She pulled out her handkerchief and valiantly attempted to dry her eyes, but it was to no avail. For every drop she wiped away three more fell. The sight of her sniffling profusely and trying to hold back her tears broke the hearts of all three men in the room; but it was Emmett's warm embrace she felt wrap her up. She sobbed into his chest, the solace he sought to provide only making her feel sadder. She could feel him patting her back soothingly as he mumbled assurances to her, but it was all for naught. She knew her fate, and she could not change it. In her time and in her land, women had no business interfering with what was to be...and for all her dignity and womanly pride, she could not stop the resignation that washed over her, a tidal wave that submerged her completely. To her, it seemed easier to breathe in the seawater and just let herself drown than to fight the undercurrents, and the temptation was great.

"All right now, Emmeline, that is quite enough." William's voice was steelier than it had been in days, his stoicism reminiscent of his past behaviour. Previously it would have irked his children, but today it only called them to attention. Emmeline straightened in her seat, daubing the wetness from her face with her soaked handkerchief. Emmett removed his arms from her and pulled away from the embrace, but kept her hands wrapped in his as they both turned to face their father.

"Tears will do nothing for our situation, my child." His voice softened slightly as he beheld her tear-stained face, and Emmeline sniffled as she nodded. He was right, and she knew it very well. "Come, now. Let us think, and solve the problem calmly. Everything will be all right, my dear, I promise you."

Emmett nodded gravely, and spoke up first. "We must act strategically. Offending the royal family would be unwise, and so we should seek, as far as possible, to avoid doing so."

"I agree," Peter said, moving to sit leaning forward with his elbows resting atop his trousered thighs and his fingers interlaced, "for, if we act imprudently, they could ruin us all."

"Perhaps we should speak to the King," the earl proposed, "and strike a deal. Perhaps, Father, if Mayfair would pledge allegiance to the throne without a marital union, the royal family would no longer need Emmeline to marry Prince Alexander. I know Mayfair has previously avoided doing so in case some unexpected situation arises, but if it is for Emmeline's sake..."

"I have been considering that as well," William agreed with a solemn nod. "It does seem like our best option at the moment. What do you think, Emmeline?"

She shifted uncomfortably in her seat. Her brother's plan did seem like the sole viable solution at the present time, but she knew it would not work. Her chances only seemed to grow bleaker with every passing minute.

"I do not mean to be a pessimist, but I do think King Andrew's mind is quite set," she said. "He loves his wife deeply – I have observed it for myself in my interactions with them. Sarah wishes me to marry her son, and now that Alexander has so blatantly defied that wish, he would never let it be any other way. He is beyond reason, and I cannot be certain that a promise of allegiance would pacify him."

William sighed. "Well, my dear, we shall have to try anyway, shall we not?"

"And if it does not work?" The trepidation was evident in Emmeline's quaking voice as she posed the question no one wished to consider, "What then?"

William was silent for a while; but he did eventually answer her:

"Then, Emmeline, I will do everything in my power to secure your happiness." A pause. "I promise you."

Chapter Nineteen - Part One

LONG AFTER EMMETT AND WILLIAM HAD RETIRED TO THEIR ROOMS, Emmeline and Peter remained in the library. After it had been decided that the foursome would visit the palace the next day to make their case to the King, the would-have-been couple had chosen to stay to talk a while longer in private. Albeit chaperoned by Penelope and one of the butlers of Wellington House for the sake of propriety, they were quite lost in each other's conversation, and both felt like they were the only two in the world. It was quite like when they danced; but without the movement and the music, the depths of the other's personality became easier to see, hear and feel. Peter seemed to smile brighter, and Emmeline's eyes sparkled with more zest. Both parties seemed, to the other, far more beautiful bathed in the light of the library chandelier and surrounded by wood, ink and silence. They spoke of their lives and their love, laughing and smiling, until Peter turned serious.

"You know, Emmeline, I proposed to you in the letter I sent – the one your brother intercepted."

"Peter..." Emmeline looked at him with pain in her bright green eyes. He had proposed to her... They could have been engaged and making wedding preparations. Emmeline had never lived a dramatic life. If there was any constancy in it at all she should have been Peter's fiancée and at this time. Instead, she found herself hearing the man she loved tell her that he had attempted a proposal she never received, while she herself was chained to another man whom she did not love, and who did not love her. This was the stuff of a dramatic opera – and while she found a substantial amount of pleasure in visiting the theatre, she did not enjoy her situation one bit.

Peter opened his mouth to speak again, but she stopped him with a shake of her head and a faint smile that showed not happiness but the ache in her heart. "Not now, my love. You can propose to me properly after I am free from the...issue with Prince Alexander."

If I am ever free from it, she added inwardly, but those words were the type that she saved for herself to marinate in. Though she longed to confess how worried she was, she kept her words firmly steered away from the undesirable outcomes that very possibly could be realised the next day. She believed that her wonderful, bright-eyed could-have-been husband-to-be did not need to know of her pessimism towards the situation.

"May at least tell you I love you?"

Emmeline choked on what would have been laughter, her emerald eyes beginning to shine both with slight amusement and with immense grief. She found herself unable to speak, but managed to nod her permission.

"I love you, Emmeline."

More tears rushed forth, and one rolled down her cheek. Swallowing the lump in her throat, she looked away to hastily wipe a runaway tear away with her embroidered handkerchief before meeting his gaze once again and forcing her throat to obey her will.

"I love you just...just as much, Peter." She paused to take a composing breath. "I will never be willing to marry anyone but you."

"And you shall never have to," he responded tenderly, resting one of his hands on hers. "Lord Mayfair will make sure of it. Just as he told you – he will do everything within his power to help."

Emmeline sighed. "I do not doubt his willingness to do so; my only concern is that rescuing me will be quite out of his means."

"If that truly is the case, Emmeline, we could elope."

"I'm afraid I don't think could ever bring myself to do so. We would have no prospects left in this land; and while I do speak Italian and Italy is a lovely place, I...I simply cannot leave my father and brother behind. They mean so much to me."

"I know," he replied, but he sounded discouraged.

"Peter..." She sounded disinclined to believe that he accepted her choice.

"I understand," he reassured her, interlacing his fingers with hers. "I do."

She smiled tightly at him, and the two were silent for a while, just holding hands and being together, before she spoke again.

"If... Whatever happens tomorrow, if I never see you again—" Emmeline's voice snagged in her throat. "Please remember I love you. Whatever happens, I will only ever love you, Peter."

She had not meant to speak of that possibility, but the thought of parting without being able to tell him of the magnitude of her love made her heart feel as if it were being crushed by the entirety of St James' Palace, and almost reluctantly she let the words out of her mouth.

"And I you," he vowed in return, his typically light hazel eyes growing thick with emotion and turning a deep shade of chocolate. "But do not cry, my love. Tomorrow will not be the last time you see me – His Grace will not let it be."

"I love you." Was all she could respond with, tears streaming down her cheeks, for they were the only words she truly knew to be true. Peter seemed so optimistic about the situation – he seemed to have so much faith in her father. Despite everything she hoped for and longed for to happen, Emmeline was all too aware that even the Duke of Mayfair had things he could not do. The probability of success, however much she did not wish to admit it, was low. Her hazel eyed captain gave her hand a comforting squeeze, though his eyes, while reassuring, conveying that he shared in her sorrow; and her heart broke, for she knew that he might not be hers for much longer.

Chapter Nineteen - Part Two

FATHER, SON, DAUGHTER AND SUITOR SAT IN A CAR-RIAGE ON THE WAY TO St James' Palace to make their appeal to the monarchs. In her anxiety, Emmeline had bitten her bottom lip to the extent of drawing blood. Peter was restless, and could not sit still. Emmett watched his sister sit by his dearest friend, and while he was fully aware of the personal price he would pay should their request be granted, he could not help but realise that they looked like a match made in heaven. Regret weighed on his chest like the self-centred worry that had once shrouded his judgement and caused great folly, but he could do naught about it but pray that the King would be merciful and reasonable. If he loved his wife as much as Emmeline claimed he did, he must understand how Emmeline and Peter felt toward one another. Surely he would not separate two young lovers so?

While all three young people in the carriage fretted, William was brooding just as much. He sat solemn and still, but if one observed his dark eyes, the concern in them was evident. He had to put on a confident front for his daughter's sake, but his most rational side told him that her worries were not unwarranted in the least.

But her mother was dead, Bethany did not care for her happiness, and the duty of securing her a life worth living fell upon his shoulders and his shoulders alone. Though they were broad, the weight of the matter was immense, and the task to accomplish was daunting even for the duke well acquainted with life's trials and tribulations. If the proposal of pledging Mayfair's allegiance to the royal family would not work, he would give everything he had to persuade the King.

The carriage eventually drew to a stop outside the Palace. A guard rapped on it and opened the door. After verifying that its passengers would not threaten security in the palace, he grumbled a pleasantry, and sent it back on its way. Another palace guard was present when the door opened again to greet them and give them directions to see the King.

Upon entry into the throne room, the three men bowed and Emmeline swept into a deep curtsy in greeting of the two regal monarchs.

"How lovely it is to see you, Duke Mayfair." Sarah greeted the duke merrily, while her husband kept deathly silent. "Who is this young man you have brought to us? What business would you like to discuss?"

"It concerns Emmeline, Your Majesty," he replied, "and the engagement."

Andrew did not look surprised, but Sarah's eyebrows raised considerably. "Oh! I see. Pray tell, my lord – if there is anything we can do to make the wedding more pleasant for you..."

"Your Majesty... I apologise in advance, but I'm afraid you could not do so," was the reply, "in any way except for calling it off."

"Call off the wedding?" she echoed with eyes wide as saucers, well and truly shocked by William's request. "Why ever would you wish for that, Lord Mayfair? Emmeline is a wonderful young lady, and it would be a blissful union—"

"Respectfully, Your Majesty, it would not be one." William's voice was grave. "Once again, I apologise, but... I'm afraid that Emmeline seems to be quite in love with another man – this young captain here. I myself had an unsuccessful marriage and I cannot—"

Halfway through his persuasive speech, however, the duke was interrupted.

"Captain, you say?" Straightening in his throne, Andrew finally spoke, his booming voice was commanding enough authority to make any man other than William Lockhart quake in his boots. He turned to Peter, his calculating eyes hawk-like as they attempted to penetrate his very soul. "You serve my navy, do you?"

Peter ordered himself to remain composed, and forced his head to nod firmly and his voice to remain level as he uttered his response. "Yes, Your Majesty."

"What is your name?"

"Peter Jamison, Your Majesty." Peter swallowed the growing lump in his throat before it could become an impediment to his speech.

"Do you have subordinates?"

"Yes, Sir."

"And what do they call you?"

"Captain Jamison, Sir."

"Captain...is a very high rank for your age. How old are you?"

"Twenty and four, Sir."

The King's eyes narrowed slightly, the cogs in his mind spinning. "You are extremely accomplished, then. You must have great passion for your occupation."

"... Yes, Your Majesty."

"Excellent," he said. "In that case, Captain Peter Jamison, should you still choose to pursue my future daughter-in-law, I will ensure that you lose your career the moment I hear of it."

Emmeline's eyes grew large with desperation. How could Peter choose between the ocean and her? He loved both. Simultaneously, how could she let herself be the cause of the loss of his career? She turned to plead with the Queen, her only hope in the face of a most resolute king. Her green eyes were beginning to water in her distress. "Sarah—"

"Sarah, my love, leave us alone to discuss this for a moment, will you?" Seeing through her strategy immediately, Andrew cut her off before she could even say the word "please".

Sarah stopped to look between her husband and the woman she had so hoped her son would marry. Her desires were one thing, but the poor lass was on the verge of tears. Although she was taken aback by the sudden request for the cancellation, and despite the slight sense of indignation she had, she felt something shift within her as she looked upon the girl who was fighting for love the way she herself had done as an adolescent.

She decided to speak. "Andrew, perhaps—"

"Enough said, Sarah. Leave us." His tone was completely unwavering, and he did not turn to look at her. This was not the first time she had seen those grey eyes so firmly fixed on a person as if he was game to be hunted – she knew that look in his eyes. Her husband was already beyond reason.

Besides, the country needed Emmeline Lockhart. None of the other can-didates who had come forth shared her wisdom, wit and proactivity. She was best for the country's future. And she was, so far, the sole individual with the exception of Greta to attempt to offer Alexander counsel when he was upset. She was the only person to ever successfully calm him draw him out of his rage-resultant reclusion – or at least, that was what the King had told Sarah.

Of course, she remained sympathetic towards Emmeline, but the young lady would find some degree of satisfaction as queen one day...would she not?

Perhaps she was not truly in love with this officer. If she was, why would he only be brought up after the engagement? Surely the young lady would have said something sooner if he meant enough to her to cancel a wedding of such scale...

She swallowed.

"Very well, Andrew. I will leave you." A pause. Then, in a lower voice, "Please be amiable to our future daughter-in-law."

She stood and left the room.

When the door closed gently behind her, Emmeline's world imploded. She felt her skull falling apart and closing into her very consciousness, and she thought she might have collapsed then and there in the throne room of St James' Palace.

It was her father's voice that summoned her back from the verge of deliri-um, and it matched Andrew's in conviction and power. "Andrew St James, I challenge you to a duel for my daughter's marriage."

"Father – no!" Emmeline cried, turning to him. "You cannot do so! I forbid it, Father, I forbid it!"

Andrew shifted in his throne, his gaze lazy and demeaning. "If I were you, Mayfair, I would listen to your daughter's counsel. As you would know, Sarah did not select her for her outer appearance."

"Stay out of this, Emmeline," William said, his voice low and firm. Yet his dark eyes. "I promised you I would secure your future. This is the only way left. Do not worry yourself excessively; I am aware of what I am doing."

"If you are aware that you are challenging the best swordsman in all the land to a duel over the small issue of one woman's marriage, Lord Mayfair, then you are less intelligent than I thought."

"However much intelligence I lack, Your Majesty." William turned to face the monarch squarely, dark eyes alight with a fire Emmeline had never seen before, "I am a father who loves his children, and I am willing to give my life for them."

Andrew observed Duke Mayfair with a slight frown, and for a long time made no reply. When he finally spoke, he said lazily,

"Well. Shall we commence the duel immediately?"

Chapter Nineteen - Part Three

A NDREW ST JAMES AND WILLIAM LOCKHART DREW THEIR SWORDS.

It was William who made the first move, but the King was every bit as skilled as he had claimed to be and deflected the move with ease. He then struck out at the duke, but William dodged the blow successfully before returning it with a counterattack. Emmeline, Emmett, Peter and Alexander – who had been summoned to witness the duel – watched nervously, all of them hoping that one particular individual would win the duel.

Yet they wished for one particular outcome for very immediate reasons and not for the further repercussions – if William won the duel, he would, automatically, overthrow the King and take his place on the throne. Yet no one paid particular attention to that detail, for no one coveted that position in the least. Their worry lay in that the spar would decide Emmeline's life and the lives of the two young suitors; beyond that, duels ended in death, and the Portsmouth twins were only fearful for their father's life, and although Alexander hardly knew the man, he was deeply worried for his prospective father-in-law. With the passing of time, his father had grown older, but seemed not to have grown old, and the prince knew that Duke Mayfair could be in real danger.

Andrew turned to the offensive, and William parried multiple blows. Yet the King seemed to only be warming up and never did slow his attack, advances raining thunderously upon William like a perfect storm. The duke seemed to begin to struggle to defend himself, his fades and retreats becoming less stable each time he moved backwards, and Emmeline grew tense in her seat at the sight of it. Emmett grasped her hand comfortingly, but she did not so much as notice him do so. She could hardly feel herself breathing – or perhaps she was no longer breathing at all.

Lunging forth, William attempted an attack at Andrew, but the monarch avoided it with a skilful sidestep, and the duke stumbled slightly from the force of his own thrust of the sword. Fortuitously he recovered speedily enough, and stood to hold his sword up at the other man in a long point, breathing heavily. His feet held him steady, but he was growing weary. Meanwhile, King Andrew had not yet so much as broken a sweat, and Emmeline knew that her father was fighting a losing battle. Her heart clenched at the thought of it, and considered surrendering herself to save her father, but her brother's hand over hers was the only thing tying her down to her seat. Perhaps there was hope yet, she told herself, perhaps the tables would turn.

William moved to strike out at his opponent once again. Andrew, with all the composure of a man confident of his swordsmanship, blocked every one of his blows, not perturbed in the least. Then, he was quick to return the attack, showering Mayfair with as many blows as he could deliver. Originally William successfully deflected each one of them, but the duke only came to be more tired with every passing second, and the battle reached a point when William was taking many steps back, almost falling, and eventually he found himself watching, frozen, as his seemingly heartless monarch drive a sword towards him at inhuman speed as the universe slowed down around him, drawing out the length of his final breathing moment.

He might have died then and there, defending his daughter's lifetime happiness in the palace courtyard if Emmeline herself had not come to his rescue. Her voice, loud and clear, halted the King as she leapt to her feet, tears in her eyes, and called out, "Enough! Stop the duel!"

The four others present turned to look at her, three of them with wide eyes, knowing the decision she had come to make. The King was the only one who did not seem shocked, and a corner of his mouth tilted upwards in something of a smug smirk. Still he kept his sword pointed menacingly at Duke Mayfair, ready to puncture his chest and take his life should she fail to say the words he wanted to hear. Emmeline swallowed in an attempt to compose herself, her hands shaking violently although she had clenched them into fists by her side. She shut her eyes, her brow furrowing involuntarily, as she attempted to breathe deeply to steel herself to the declaration she was about to make. She could not bring herself to look at her brother or the man whom she loved, the man who had proposed to her but would not marry her after all.

A tear escaped her shining emerald eyes and rolled down her cheek as she raised her head once more, glaring most hatefully at the King, and announced with as much conviction as grief, "Stop the duel! I will marry the prince...I will marry him!"

The King finally relaxed, a slight satisfied smile coming to rest upon his lips, and his sword clattered to the floor. "Very good, lass. It does seem after all that you are as wise as my wife thinks you are. I will deliver Sarah the good news."

With that, he quit the palace courtyard, and Emmeline hitched up her skirts to run as quickly as she could to her father, throwing her arms around him, resting her neck over his right shoulder and dissolving into a fit of sobs. "Father – oh, Father..."

He rested a hand on her back, regret washing over him as he closed his eyes to keep himself from shedding tears as well. He had not expected King Andrew to be so skilled, and he had not expected to have grown rusty in his swordsmanship from decades of a lack of necessity to fight. "I – I am sorry, Emmeline. I did not think..."

"No – no, Father," she managed to choke out, pulling back to meet his eyes as she sloppily wiped the tears from her face with the backs of her hands. "None of this is your fault... You should not have taken the risk – what would I do without you? How could you risk your life so?"

Emmett watched his sister embrace his father once more as she began to weep profusely, and felt a twisting feeling in his stomach. Yet he was rooted to the spot, and could not move to comfort her.

More than that, he could not bring himself to look at Peter.

Chapter Twenty

<hr>

NOT MORE THAN THREE MONTHS AFTER THE CALLING AN END TO HER father's duel with the King, Lady Emmeline Artemis Lockhart was dressed in a white gown, her face covered – almost caked – with powder and rouge and various other colourings, her hair braided and twisted painfully tight. She felt as if she were not a real human being. Penelope had not been the one to style her – instead, Bethany had sent for a professional to make her into a doll for her wedding ceremony.

A thin white veil masked her pained expression as she sat in front of her dressing table, looking at herself and thinking of the life she had enjoyed, the life she could have had, the life she might no longer live. St James' Palace was a gilded cage – she would be a princess and one day queen, but she would lose many of her small pleasures. She did not know if her fingers would touch the fingerboard of a violoncello again. She did not know if she would be able to see Adalberto frequently, if she would, whenever she wanted to, be able to see his smile and his kind fatherly eyes and hear him call her piccola signorina. Her life would be one cast under public scrutiny, and the small joys of privacy she used to relish so much were slipping through her fingers faster than she could attempt to catch onto them. Sitting in her breathtaking white gown, her face made up to be far more attractive than it truly was, Emmeline Lockhart wanted to weep. For the three months leading to her wedding day, she had felt as if she were grasping at straws; all those days had culminated in this peak, the one day that everything she knew and loved would finally disappear from her altogether.

Yet, as she awaited helplessly the death of the life she knew and loved, she made a valiant attempt to remain somewhat optimistic: she told herself that this issue was bigger than herself; she attempted to persuade herself that it was not all bad. She was, after all, doing a service to her country, committing her intelligence and all her good judgement to the wellbeing of her great kingdom. She told herself that her marriage was a way of solidifying ties between Mayfair and the Crown, so that her father and brother would never fall out of favour with the ruling family. Her own place in the royal family would also mean that she would now be able to offer assistance she had never been able to give. She begged herself to remember – to believe – that her newfound royal status would also signify that she would have more individual agency. As princess, her words would carry more weight, her name would carry more authority, and her actions would carry more meaning. She pleaded with her subconscious to accept the notion that all this was for the better.

Regardless of what she willed her mind to turn to, all it wanted to think of was Peter. Her Captain Peter Jamison, her hazel-eyed hero, her lover and friend, the one man who could have made her happy. The sailor in love with the sea but more in love with her... The man who was probably spending the most important day of her life mourning. She had been meant to marry him – she had been fated to. She knew it as a fact that they were designed to be together. He was supposed to be the one preparing to be married to Lady Emmeline Lockhart. He was supposed to be the one to stand by her at the altar and say that he loved her... He was supposed to be her husband, her one and only for all her life. Yet the one getting ready for the wedding ceremony at a nearby venue was not Captain Jamison but His Royal Highness Prince Alexander, a man who did not want to marry her, a man whom she did not want to marry, a man whom she had no affinity with nor love for. And Peter Jamison, the man of her dreams, was likely in an upscale inn in London not too far away drowning his sorrows in hard liquor – for the love of his life was about to marry another man, for the love of his life would one day be queen of a kingdom he was not heir to. She could imagine him sitting forlornly, hazel eyes clouded not with drunkenness but with sorrow, holding back tears he should not have to shed. She could feel the ache in his heart, the ache she shared. For they would not see each other for a long time to come. His Majesty King Andrew had specifically stated that Peter Jamison was disallowed from seeking the prospective princess, and though her heart had shattered at the declaration, Emmeline had only been able to grit her teeth and hide her tears, choking back sobs.

"My lady." Penelope Smith's voice was quiet behind her. "It is time."

"Penny... I do not love him." Her voice was choked, and her maid in waiting felt a fresh wave of sadness and sympathy wash over her. Lady Emmeline had done nothing to deserve such a tragic fate. She had always been nothing but kind and good... And yet how many kind and good women were victims of marriages forced upon them? There was no way of knowing, but Penny knew that there were too many.

"I know." A gentle hand was laid on Emmeline's shoulder in an attempt at consolation. "I will never leave your side, my lady. I will serve you until we both turn grey with age."

Emmeline managed to force a laugh at the thought of growing old. "Thank you, Penelope. If not for you...I would be all alone."

"I would never allow that." Behind her, the young maid smiled, though she herself was barely grown. "Now we truly must go, my lady. We will be late if we do not leave immediately."

Emmeline stood, shaky on her legs, and Penelope helped her out of the room, leading her through numerous hallways and finally coming to stand before the doors that would lead to the church hall. William had been awaiting her there, and came to greet her with open arms.

"You look beautiful today, my dearest."

"Father..." Tears sprang to her eyes again as she rushed into his embrace. "Oh, Father..."

"I wish I could do more for you, Emmeline. I—"

Emmeline interrupted him, perhaps meaning to come across as assertive, but she sounded nothing but pained, the heartbreak was clear in her voice. "This is not your fault, Father, but I...I just wish it did not have to be this way."

Lord Mayfair tightened his arms around her, trying his hardest to provide the fatherly warmth he had failed to give for so many years of his children's lives."As do I, my dearest. I am sorry."

"I will miss you dearly, Father," she choked out.

He shut his eyes tightly to stop his own tears from falling. "I promise I will come to see you as often as I can – remember that Wellington House is not far from the palace at all, my dear. And I am certain your brother does not mind the distance between Portsmouth and London one bit."

"Will I be all right, Father?" she asked, and he could hear the trepidation in her tone. "Regardless of what happens?"

"Of course, Emmeline. You will be just fine. A princess – think of it!"

"A princess," she echoed with a chuckle. She knew that her father was only trying to lighten her mood, but her laughter emerged from her coloured lips tired, dry and devoid of any humour. The thought of being princess was not appealing to her at all. She yearned not to be royalty but to be lady of a ship, standing atop a wooden deck with her true beloved. Yet it was not to be.

"What if the castle bores me to death?" she asked, doing her best to hold back her tears so that she would not ruin the artwork drawn upon her face as she thought of being driven to insanity by the restrictive nature of her new life.

"Then you will come away from it," he answered comfortingly, every word a solemn promise. "I will come to fetch you myself, or I might write your brother and he will take you away. Only for a short while, perhaps, but he will take you away..."

The time father and daughter had to share before Emmeline Lockhart changed her name was far from indefinite, however, and soon the doors they were to walk through opened. William led Emmeline down the aisle, her hand tucked in the crook of his elbow, tears stinging in her eyes behind her white veil, and handed her to Prince Alexander, who greeted her with a sad smile. She returned the gesture, although she did not know if he could see it or her shining eyes through her veil. She said her vows with a voice as steady as she could manage, pleading with her throat not to betray that she was on the verge of tears as she gave her life to this man she did not love and this man who did not want her as his bride. Prince Alexander made his promises in return, sounding just as agonised although his eyes remained dry. When the priest announced that anyone with protest should speak then or forever hold their peace, Emmeline Lockhart held her breath, hoping she might hear her beloved calling out that he was in love with her, that no one else would ever have her heart. That he had protest to this marriage. That she was meant to be with him, that he was supposed to be standing on that altar. She closed her eyes and prayed that he would come to take her away, to save her despite everything, despite the choice she had had to make. That he would still, in the end, be hers.

Alas, Peter Jamison never came.

With no other protest against this "lovely union between two young people in love", the priest declared them man and wife, the guests cheered, and the lady who had now become a princess felt her heart break anew. She would never be Lady Emmeline Lockhart again. Princess Emmeline. She tried to swallow the doubt forming as a lump in her throat. The title next to her name sounded wrong for too many reasons, none of which she was able to articulate. As they stood together on the altar, now husband and wife, Prince Alexander gazed sympathetically upon her, knowing the man on her mind was not him. She did not notice, for she was wrapped up in her own rumination, marinating in all the thoughts of what if and if only – thoughts that could make a man go mad.

What if Emmett had never viewed Peter as such a threat? What if Bethany had not been so eager? What if Emmeline had been more willing to throw a fit? Knowing that asking these questions would be of no benefit to her now, she sighed. If only Emmett had not begged Bethany's help, if only she herself had been firmer, if only Peter had expressed his interest sooner, if only William had taken action, if only Emmett had been willing to help, if only Prince Alexander had been less brash... If only so many insignificant mistakes had not been made, she thought, the worst day of Emmeline's life might have been her best.

***

HER MAJESTY QUEEN EMMELINE HAD, ON HER WEDDING DAY, FOUND herself unable to visualise the aging process.

Yet she had aged. Time had passed, and she had grown old. Her jet black hair had turned silver and grey, wrinkles stretching out upon her face like the shadows of time during the sunset. For the first time she felt lucky not to have much prettiness to lose; rather, she seemed to only have become even more beautiful with the passing of time, the wisdom in her pale green eyes lending her a kind of fairylike mystique she found herself quite fond of.

Presently she was seated in her study, poring over a military proposal. Her husband King Alexander had entrusted most of these proposals to her to vet and evaluate, for she had, over the years, proven herself to have a excellent judgement in the field of national defence. Her lady in waiting Penelope Smith stood close by, watching her queen toil, periodically pouring more tea into the cup that seemed to automatically drain itself as Emmeline worked without rest.

There was a rap on the door.

"Come in," the Queen called out, not looking up.

Sh raised her eyes only when a footman stepped into the room and bowed deeply. "Your Majesty – there is a guest to see you."

"What business has this guest with me?"

"He is an admiral in our Royal Navy, Madam, and wishes to report to you on the last approved proposal."

"Should he not seek out King Alexander's audience instead?" she asked pointedly. "Please redirect this admiral to His Majesty."

"I'm afraid not, Madam. His Majesty issued an order not long ago that all such reports should come directly to you."

Emmeline fought the urge to roll her eyes and nodded instead, her resignation clear as she sighed heavily. "I see. Very well, then. Kindly send this admiral to the main drawing room; I will listen to his report there."

"Yes, Your Majesty."

She nodded once more with a faint smile. "Thank you."

The footman bowed and retreated.

After he had made himself scarce, Emmeline gathered her skirts and stood with a sigh. "Come, Penelope." As the two made their way to the drawing room, she complained, "Alexander is as ridiculous as ever – how could he order the staff of his military to report directly to me? I do not mind going over his proposals and bringing my ideas to him, but it is hardly proper – by society's standards anyway – for a woman to command officers directly. What a preposterous notion."

The lady in waiting laughed. "I think it a sign of trust."

"Perhaps, but I think giving idle tongues such an opportunity to wag is likely a sign of idiocy, also," she remarked in return, and then two laughed together.

Emmeline stepped into the drawing room, and the admiral stood to greet her. She froze in place when she saw his face. He bowed deeply, as if he did not notice her shock. "Good afternoon, Your Majesty."

"Rise," she said, but her voice was soft and her breathing tight.

He obeyed, and smiled at her with his eyes twinkling.

His eyes—

She would know those hazel eyes anywhere.

*** THE END ***